Rants and Raves for Steve Burt

He's *baaaaaack!* Yup, it's Tomb Fave Steve Burt, back again with *Oddest Yet,* nine charming, disarming—and yes, *alarming*—tales guaranteed to put a chill on the hottest summer night. Gather 'round the campfire or drag a flashlight under the bed-covers with you for a scary clandestine trip to Stephen King's house in "Storming Stephen King's". Read a truly frightening collection of life-and-death correspondence between two siblings who truly understand "The Power of the Pen". Take a dark ride to "The French Acre", where restless spirits roam the dark landscape. Strangeness abounds between the covers of this book, again beautifully illustrated by the Jessica Hagerman. Collect all three of these titles to share with all ages with a predilection for weirdness. Your kids will love these stories and so will you! Highly recommended.

— J.L. COMEAU, EDITOR/TOMBKEEPER, *THE CREATURE FEATURE REVIEW PAGE,* WWW.COUNTGORE.COM

Steve Burt's work keeps you guessing with a savvy blend of unusual characters and unexpected situations. Just when you think you have the story cornered, you'll find it's sneaked up and gripped you by the back of the neck instead.

— BILL HUGHES, EDITOR, *DREAD MAGAZINE*

Steve Burt has a taste for chilling the heart. His prose is genuine, well constructed, and relies more on atmosphere and skillful plotting than blood and gore, making his stories old-fashioned in the best sense of the term. If you think, "they just don't write them like that anymore," you'll be pleased to discover that Burt does.

— GARRETT PECK, *THE HELLNOTES BOOK REVIEW*

When I teach high school seniors story-writing in a Writing-to-Publish class, I always include Steve Burt's Stories to Chill the Heart series of books (*Odd Lot, Even Odder, Oddest Yet,* and *Wicked Odd*) in the mystery/suspense examples. Teens know the real thing when they read it, and Burt's characters ring true. His stories are the next best thing to camping in the woods, listening to the distant howl of wolves and wondering if that strange midnight smell might be blood.

— MARYLIN WARNER, PAST PRESIDENT, PIKE'S PEAK BRANCH, NATIONAL LEAGUE OF AMERICAN PEN WOMEN

If ever there was an author to rival the storytelling genius of M.R. James and E.F. Benson, Steve Burt is it. Eerie and compelling, Burt's prose will have you relishing those lonely places where light dare not tread.

— DON H. LAIRD, PUBLISHER, *CROSSOVER PRESS, THRESHOLD MAGAZINE*

Steve Burt enthralled our 6th through 8th grade students. The stories ignited much discussion in every class. These are stories that kids want to read and talk about! Kids are asking for his books and want to know when we can have him back. Teachers told me what a great day it was. The most successful author visit we've ever had.

— FRAN JOHNSON, LIBRARY/MEDIA SPECIALIST, NEWFOUND MEMORIAL MIDDLE SCHOOL, BRISTOL, NH

Steve Burt has a firm grasp of the unsettling and the uncanny. His stories are set in a recognizable world, but they never go in the obvious direction, preferring instead to take off down dark alleys and twisting roads which leave the reader shivering and looking nervously into dark corners when the book is closed.

— BARBARA RODEN, EDITOR, *ALL HALLOWS* (THE MAGAZINE OF THE GHOST STORY SOCIETY)

Odd Lot and Even Odder are creepy, grisly, ghostly tales you can share with your kids and, if you're a kid, share with your parents. Spooktacularly entertaining summertime reading. Highly recommended.

— J.L. COMEAU, EDITOR, *CREATURE FEATURE TOMB*
www.countgore.com

Still More Stories to Chill the Heart

STEVE BURT

Illustrations by Jessica Hagerman

Burt Creations

Norwich, CT

Wicked Odd
Still More Stories to Chill the Heart

FIRST EDITION 2005
Second Printing, 2005

ISBN-10 0-9741-4072-4
ISBN-13 978-0-9741-4072-8

Printed in USA

Inquiries should be addressed to:

Burt Creations

Steve Burt
29 Arnold Place
Norwich, CT 06360

T 860 889-4066
F 860 889-4068

www.burtcreations.com

Illustrations by Jessica Hagerman
Design by Dotti Albertine

Also by Steve Burt

Oddest Yet, Even More Stories to Chill the Heart
Burt Creations 2004

Even Odder, More Stories to Chill the Heart
Burt Creations 2003

Odd Lot, Stories to Chill the Heart
Burt Creations 2001

A Christmas Dozen
Burt Creations 2000 (paperback)
2001 (audiobook) 2002 (hardcover)

The Little Church That Could
Judson Press 2000

Unk's Fiddle
Steven E. Burt 1995 (hardcover)
Burt Creations 2001 (paperback)

What Do You Say to a Burning Bush?
CSS Publishing 1995

My Lord, He's Loose in the World!
Brentwood Christian Press 1994

Raising Small Church Esteem
with Hazel Roper
Alban Institute 1992

Christmas Special Delivery
Fairway Press 1991

Fingerprints on the Chalice
CSS Publishing 1990

Activating Leadership in the Small Church
Judson Press 1988

Awards

WINNER, **Bram Stoker Award for Young Readers**, Horror Writers Association

NOMINEE/FINALIST, **Bram Stoker Award for Young Readers**, Horror Writers Association

SILVER MEDAL, **Benjamin Franklin Award Best Mystery/Suspense Book**
Publishers Marketing Association

FINALIST, **Best Juvenile/Young Adult Fiction**
ForeWord Magazine Book of the Year Awards

SOLE HONORABLE MENTION, **Best Horror**
ForeWord Magazine Book of the Year Awards

RUNNER-UP, **Best Genre Fiction**, *Writer's Digest*
10th International Self-Published Book Awards

RUNNER-UP, **Best Inspirational,** *Writer's Digest*
10th International Self-Published Book Awards

FINALIST, **Best Adult Audio Fiction**
ForeWord Magazine Book of the Year Awards

3 **Ray Bradbury Creative Writing Awards**

7 HONORABLE MENTIONS
Year's Best Fantasy & Horror

CONTENTS

Thanks to

...Jessica Hagerman for the great cover art and illustrations. Jessie has done all four books in the Stories to Chill the Heart series.

...Dotti Albertine at Albertine Book Design for designing the interior of these books, and for taking my basic ideas and Jessie's artwork and transforming them into fantastic front and back covers.

...Laren Bright, copywriter extraordinaire, for his skills and passion with words.

...Ellen Reid of Little Moose Press, Smarketing.com, and BookShepherding.com, who is undoubtedly the top Book Shepherd in the business, for hanging in with me since the beginning.

...Jo Ann Burt, my wife, who keeps letting me do these weird books, and who doesn't quit her day job, thank God.

...Wendy Burt, my daughter, who is not only a topnotch professional editor and award-winning writer herself, but is somehow able to be the dispassionate First Reader and later Final Editor for her Dad's work. Her tender ruthlessness makes the stories much better.

...The Horror Writers Association for its extravagant gesture of support in voting this book's two predecessors, *Even Odder* and *Oddest Yet,* Nominee/Finalists for the 2003 and 2004 **Bram Stoker Awards for Young Readers.** (In doing so, they also gave me the dubious distinction of being the only ordained minister ever to win horror's top award, and the only self-published book to do so in the Young Readers category.)

...Steven Pressfield for his prodding book, *The War of Art.*

About the Author

Steve Burt grew up in Greenport, New York, a farming and fishing village on Long Island's North Fork. He and his cousins and friends dug tunnels, built tree houses, ran away from home a few times, leapfrogged across the rooftops of village stores, explored the underground storm drain system, and clubbed hordes of marauding rats at the local dump. With so many adventures during the day, no wonder he had weird dreams at night. And now that he's an adult, it all comes out in the weird tales kids and adults love in his Stories to Chill the Heart Series.

About the Artist

JESSICA E. HAGERMAN is a freelance illustrator who works primarily in pen and ink. She lives in Massachusetts with her cat and dog. Jessie has done the cover art and illustrations for all four books in the Stories to Chill the Heart Series: *Odd Lot, Even Odder, Oddest Yet*, and *Wicked Odd.* In addition to illustrating CD jackets, books, and occasional medical articles, Jessie uses her degree in Art Therapy to work with children at the Shriners Children's Hospital in Springfield, Massachusetts. In February 2005 she was the Coordinator and sole Spanish interpreter for a group called Healing the Children, which made a mission trip to Ecuador to offer free surgery to children with cleft palates and similar problems. Jessie also plays guitar and sings, and is co-proprietor of Peaceful Products.

About the Stories

None of the stories in *Wicked Odd* have been previously published. They are all original to this collection. Because people ask about the background and origin of different stories at my read-aloud sessions, I thought I'd share a little about each.

"Croaker" was written in February-March-April 2005 and is kind of the way I remember my second visit to the Methodist camp, Quinipet, on Shelter Island. (I actually went to camp there once, and that was fifth or sixth grade.)

"The Cave" is one I recorded out of thin air in February 2003 while walking my dog Opie, figuring I'd use it in *Even Odder.* But a month later when I went to transcribe it, the audiotape was blank. I had hit Play, not Record. Curses, I hate it when that happens. So I jotted down the idea in a sentence and, because I was under a tight deadline for *Even Odder,* moved ahead without it. I got back to writing it from the one-sentence summary in April 2005.

"Night Train to Plantation 13" was my way of getting back to rural Maine. Except that the rural Maine in this story is far more isolated and bizarre than where I lived. The first page was a journal jotting in 2004, but the story stalled. Over the next year the details began to come together in my head, though very slowly. It wasn't until I came across a terrific short book about procrastination, Steven Pressfield's *The War of Art*, that I finally buckled down and wrote it in the winter of 2005.

"The Tattooist" gave me a chance to see Uncle Bando again. Readers loved him in "Uncle Bando's Chimes" (*Oddest Yet*) and wanted more of him. The part about the break-in, the wine cellar, getting caught, trying to run away to Florida, getting stuck in Elizabeth, New Jersey, is true. But in real life, the guy in the Volvo ratted us out to the cops, who surrounded the car and took us to the station, where they held us until our irate fathers arrived in the wee hours of the morning to get us. There was hell to pay when we got home.

"The Chair" shows my fascination with the paranormal and such concepts as telekinesis, clairvoyance, and clairaudience. In 2003 I read a book about a famous police psychic who lives a few blocks from me, so I dictated "The Chair" during a walk. But as with "The Cave," I had punched Play instead of Record and ended up with a blank tape. Again I jotted down the idea in a long sentence, and in Spring 2005, finally got back to it.

"The Chambers Crypt" is my third paranormal mystery with Devaney and Hoag, two "ghost busters" who investigate weird happenings around Norwich, Vermont (up the road from where I lived in White River Junction). They first appeared in "The Witness Tree" (*Odd Lot*) then in "The French Acre" (*Oddest Yet*).

A Word About the Word "Wicked"

I promised fans I'd explain the regional slang word *wicked*—as in *wicked odd, wicked funny, wicked smart, wicked stupid, wicked awful,* and those summer signs on Cape Cod proclaiming *Wicked Good Chowdah.*

It comes from Northern New England, *wicked* does, and I first heard it myself in the 1970s in rural Maine and northern New Hampshire. Then in the 1980s I discovered it had infected northern Vermont and was starting to creep across Lake Champlain into northeastern New York State. By the 1990s *wicked* could be found in coastal Massachusetts. I heard and saw it regularly at my book signings on Cape Cod and knew it was approaching epidemic proportions. (I wasn't the carrier, though, I swear. I'm simply telling where I've encountered it.)

Wicked is an adverb, a silly sort of modifier that simply means *very*, or *very very*, or *really*, or *extremely*. Try substituting those words for *wicked* and you'll see what I mean, how easy to use and how much fun it is. At first your version may not sound as colorful, but keep at it; it'll come.

At book signings, when I'd tell people that the fourth book in my series would be titled *Wicked Odd*, it was easy to spot the New Englanders—they were the ones who laughed right away and heartily—but everyone else—especially Midwesterners and those from Bible Belt states, for whom the word *wicked* has a very different connotation—stared blankly as if I'd told an inside joke that they weren't in on.

When I told my book designer and my agent (both from the West Coast), I got the modified Midwest response. Silence. Even after I explained it and they said they got it, they didn't laugh. They said, "But nobody outside New England is going to get it! What're you going to do, educate the rest of the world about *wicked?*"

"Good idea," I said. "I will. And once they get it, they'll love saying it. As you say, it's a challenge, *but, like, you know*, it'll be wicked fun."

Introduction

WHERE DO THESE WEIRD TALES COME FROM? Whether it's at a read-aloud session for middle school kids, a storytelling program at a senior center or library, or a how-to-write workshop at a conference, the question always comes up: *Where do you get your ideas?*

There are many answers. Here are a few.

Childhood memories and experiences. Did you ever run away from home, or threaten to, or at least think about doing it? The first time I did, I was six or seven, and my mother said that I packed three pairs of underwear and several bars of soap—nothing else. I only got a couple hundred yards from home. The next time I was ten, and my cousin and I went so far as to lift the key to his father's boat. But we aborted the mission when we realized we couldn't read nautical maps and lacked gas money. Then, when I was barely a teenager, three of us started hitch-hiking to Florida for orange-picking jobs, but got caught in Elizabeth, New Jersey. Not all that interesting, these three anecdotes, but what happens when, as an adult writer, I ask this question: What really bizarre, dark-side adventure *might* happen to runaways? (Hint: Check out "The Tattooist," the fourth story in this book.)

Consider how the many Steve/Chuck/Spider/Ramon stories in my series came about. From childhood memories: ice skating parties on a cemetery pond ("The Skating Party" in *Even Odder*), swimming in an oyster-boat basin ("The Swimmer" in *Oddest Yet*), exploring the storm drains under the village ("Beneath the Streets" in *Even Odder*), summer camp ("Croaker," the opening story in this book), digging tunnels, ("Too Deep" in *Oddest Yet*), walking past a scarecrow and a private cemetery ("Garden Plot" in *Odd Lot*). It's not so much what *happened* as what *could have happened,* and there's the story.

Reading. I have yet to meet a good writer who doesn't read voraciously. Reading usually produces ideas. Just because one person wrote a tale about vampires (*Dracula*, by Bram Stoker), that doesn't mean everything's been said about them. Consider Anne Rice's *The Vampire Lestat* or *The Vampire Chronicles*. Two different *Dark Shadows* TV series, about the vampire Barnabas, were hits. Then there's *Buffy the Vampire Slayer,* which is both a hit TV show and a book series. There's plenty of other vampire material, too, and although there's so much of it, it's successful because readers enjoy the characters and stories. ("Vampire" in *Even Odder* is a coming-of-age/puberty story.)

Myself, I love to read, and I gobble down hundreds of short stories every year. There are plenty of horror *collections* to be found on bookstore shelves (collection usually means many stories by a single author). There are also many horror *anthologies* out there (anthology indicates many stories by different authors). One story I read was about a practical joke gone horribly wrong, and that got me to wondering—what kind of practical joke can I come up with that can backfire on some characters ("Captain James's Bones" in *Odd Lot*)? When I'm teaching writing in schools, I tell kids not to worry so much about creating something totally new and original. That's a lot of pressure on someone just starting out in writing. What's wrong with reading a story and writing something similar? It's been said, "imitation is the sincerest form of flattery." So use a story as a model, but don't plagiarize, don't copy it word for word and say it's yours. We can learn by imitating, and in time create our own new stories.

Now when I say to read, I don't mean it has to be short fiction or even fiction at all. One year I read about Uri Geller, the Israeli mentalist, and was so fascinated by his being able to manipulate metal with his mind that I wrote "The Spoonbender" (*Even Odder*), about a girl who could do the same but grew too cocky about her abilities.

Over the years I enjoyed several articles and nonfiction books about the Underground Railroad that escaped slaves traveled, and about the strange hiding places (hidden panels and tunnels in homes, for example), and these stimulated me to create "The Chambers Crypt" (the final novella in this collection).

Life experience. When my wife and I lived in South Bristol, Maine in 1998-1999, we'd walk our dog every night near the famous Pemaquid Point Lighthouse. We climbed on the rocks below, saw and heard the waves crashing, felt the spray, and listened to tales about shipwrecks. How could we not think of ghosts? Then one day I read a gripping story in *Yankee Magazine* about rogue waves that had snatched tourists off the rocks while they were viewing the surf. Shortly after that, I was at the lighthouse (the interior of which is closed to the public) while the Coast Guard was performing annual maintenance. I introduced myself and got a free guided tour, including an inspection and explanation of the huge Fresnel lens in the tower. With all those ingredients, all I needed was the right characters and motivations for a classic ghost story ("Lighthouse Moths" in *Odd Lot*).

Likewise, "The French Acre" (*Oddest Yet*) started with *place*. Every day when I walked my dog through an historic cemetery in Norwich (Connecticut), we'd pass this marker with twenty miniature French flags around it. They marked the sacrifice of twenty of Lafayette's French soldiers who died while stationed at Norwich during the American Revolution. About the time I discovered the monument and flags, my ghost-hunting detectives Devaney and Hoag from Norwich (Vermont) were begging for a fresh case. So I wove together the two Norwiches and manufactured another twenty soldiers (only these were British).

Your fears. Whenever I saw people ice fishing and snowmobiling on the (maybe) frozen lakes and rivers of Vermont and Maine, I worried they'd might fall through and drown. (My cousin Chuck once broke through thin ice on a pond we dared each other to walk on, and we almost didn't get him out.) So I had my fears and needed to create a story about them. The challenge in "The Ice Fisherman" (*Odd Lot*) was how to turn an ice-hole drowning into a positive thing.

"Uncle Bando's Chimes" (*Oddest Yet*) was my way of dealing with three fears: New York City subways, bullies, and gangs. It was a justice-be-done story. But stories about our fears don't always need to have happy endings or satisfactory resolutions. "Chancey's Puppetry" (*Even Odder*), for example, was a fun story, but it didn't change my creepy feelings about dummies, clowns, and manikins. Nor did "Carousel" (*Even Odder*) wipe the demonic grins off those merry-go-round horses' faces.

Suggestions from others. Last year when I was scrounging for ideas, my wife said, "We used to live practically next door to Stephen King in Bangor. Why don't you write a story about that creepy house of his?" I did, "Storming Stephen King's" (*Oddest Yet*). Thanks, Honey.

So where do ideas come? Everywhere: childhood memories, reading, life experience, our fears, suggestions from others. It's not so much about *where* the ideas come from; it's about *training ourselves* to uncover them, to mine them, to experiment with them.

Somebody once said a writer is someone who sees a story behind every tree. How about every stone? Imagine this. After your grandfather's death, you are called in to repair the stone wall in his back pasture. But to repair it, you must first take out a bunch of the stones. What or who do you find *beneath* the removed stones? What or who do you find *behind* the wall? What clings to the stones and gets onto your hands, and with what result? What can you do with just one of those stones? How does any of this affect your life or the life of your character(s)? Do things get corrected or do they get worse? On the surface this looks like a person repairing a stone wall, but you can choose to make it into something more. (Read Edgar Allen Poe's *The Cask of Amontillado.*) There are many stories waiting to be uncovered. So, go ahead, entertain me, I dare you.

CROAKER

THE WHOLE CROAKER THING started and ended with the North Ferry.

It was a Sunday morning in early August and the four of us—my cousins Chuck and Spider, our best friend Ramon and I—were waiting near the North Ferry in Greenport for the church buses that would take us to Quinipet, the Methodist retreat center on Shelter Island, for a week of summer camp. The other campers and counselors would be coming from New York City, other parts of Long Island, and western Connecticut. But we four lived right across the bay from Shelter Island in Greenport, the final bus pickup point. After a ten-minute ferry ride and a ten-minute bus ride on Shelter Island, we'd be there.

"This better be good," Ramon said as the first of six buses rounded the corner of Front and Third and came into sight.

Chuck, Spider, and Ramon had never been to camp. They were doing it on my recommendation. My sister Nancy and I had gone the year before. I'd been eleven, she ten. We'd had a great week and talked about it for months after. Now she was at a different camp somewhere up the Hudson River.

"Can't wait to paddle a war canoe," Spider said.

Spider and I had been at the Greenport docks earlier in the summer when a bunch of counselors-in-training broke the rules and paddled across the bay in them. The canoes were huge, oversized on both ends. One was

painted like a South Seas war canoe, another like a Viking long ship. The third had an outrigger, a pontoon, out to the side. The groups my sister and I had been in the year before weren't allowed to use them—something about age and insurance—but I was pretty sure we'd get a chance this year. It was the main selling point I'd used to convince Chuck, Spider, and Ramon to sign up for camp.

The buses swung into the ferry line to wait for the next boat. The first five buses were jammed with kids, but the sixth was only three-quarters full, so we climbed on it.

"Hey, Dante," I said, high-fiving a kid I recognized from the year before. "Good to see you back, buddy. How's life in Poughkeepsie?"

I introduced Chuck, Ramon, and Spider to Dante, who in turn introduced other kids to us. Several were camp veterans, others newbies.

"I'm sure you heard about Croaker, right?" Dante said.

Chuck, Ramon, and Spider knew who Dante was referring to. I had filled them in. The man everybody called Croaker—his real name was Kroeker or Kroeger or Kroener, something like that—was Quinipet's long-time handyman. He was a tall, muscular blond with a deep voice and always wore a blue New York Yankees jacket. He had a trace of a German accent, and people around the camp swore he was a World War II German soldier who couldn't get into Argentina, so he was trying to lie low on Shelter Island. Everyone agreed that he was rude, arrogant, and unfriendly. He ordered campers around like they were slaves. Except for the Camp Manager, the caretaker was the only year-round resident position at the camp. Apparently he got his room, board, and a small salary in exchange for mowing lawns, plowing snow, maintaining the buildings, and taking care of

the waterfront—meaning the swimming float, lifeguard towers, picnic tables, sailboats, and war canoes. His cabin door said PRIVATE, KEEP OUT. THIS MEANS YOU. Croaker was a scary dude. He meant it.

"No," I said. "I haven't heard a thing. What about him?"

"He's gone," Dante said. "Packed all his stuff up in the middle of the night, I hear, about a month before the first week of orientation for counselors. Nobody's sure exactly when. He didn't give notice. Just split, headed for parts unknown."

I was tempted to say, "Good riddance," but instead said, "You're kidding!"

Ramon joked, "What happened—Feds get wind of him?"

"Nobody knows," Dante said. "He must have hitchhiked or left on foot."

"What makes you say that?" Chuck asked.

"Because he had no car, at least not one of his own. Didn't need one. He drove the camp maintenance truck to get around the island. And he never left Shelter Island, at least not so far as anyone ever saw. My dad was a counselor for years, and he said Croaker was more than just a hermit. It was like he was afraid to leave the island. Anyhow, he didn't take the camp truck."

"Then we should cheer up, right?" Ramon said, grinning. "Good riddance to bad rubbish?"

We laughed, and Ramon, having an audience now, pretended to raise a glass.

"A toast," he said, and we all hoisted imaginary champagne glasses. "To Croaker's replacement, may she be eighteen and a swimsuit model."

We laughed again, and Spider fudged a British accent saying, "Here, here," and everyone pretended to drink. But something didn't feel right.

☾☾☾

"Be sure you've got all your gear from the buses," squawked someone on a bullhorn. The instructions came from a scrawny, middle-aged man standing on a picnic table. He wore a fluorescent yellow windbreaker, and in the V of the jacket's neck I could see an oversized wooden cross hanging from a rawhide thong. He held a clipboard under his arm and was trying too hard to look and sound important. The cap on his head was navy blue, and his ponytail stuck out the back of it. Gold lettering over the brim declared him SUPREME COMMANDER.

"That's Mr. Tinker, the Camp Manager," I said. "He's got this control thing. Behind his back you might call him Tink or Tinker or even Tinkerbell, but to his face it's *Mr. Tinker*. I don't know who was harder to get along with—him or Croaker."

"Hey, those two barely tolerated each other," Dante interrupted. "No love lost there."

After we'd gotten into our groups, Tinker took to his bullhorn and began droning out instructions about the facilities, mealtimes and procedures, recreation, quiet time, worship time, arts and crafts time, and free time.

A kid raised his hand. "Mr. Tinker, you forgot to mention waterfront. What about swim time, sailboats, and the war canoes?"

Tinker put on a sad face. "I hate to break it to you, kiddies, but don't unpack your bathing suits this week. All summer we've had reports of sharks in the waters near the swimming area. So, in the interest of everyone's safety, I've closed the waterfront for the season. No swimming, no sailing, no canoeing." He didn't even say he was sorry.

A collective groan went up and the grumbling started.

"Quiet. Quiet down," Tinker called out. "I know you're disappointed. But I'm sure your parents and your pastors would prefer my closing the beach to risking their children's lives. Don't you agree?"

"No war canoes?" Ramon grumbled. "Sharks can't get you inside the boat."

"Do you think your parents would let you take the war canoes out with sharks in the waters?" Tinker said in his best shaming voice.

Ramon shot me a dirty look. "Damn. No war canoes."

"Hey," I said with a defensive shrug. "How could I know?"

We were so disappointed we barely heard the rest of Tinker's instructions.

☾☾☾

By Thursday the four of us were sick and tired of Half-a-Camp, as Spider put it. Sure, softball and arts-and-crafts time were fun. And the hikes around other parts of Shelter Island were OK, especially the visit our cabin made (there were seven of us and our counselor) to the Old Quaker Burying Ground. There we had lunch on log benches in an outdoor meeting circle and afterwards poked around a bunch of old graves in the middle of the woods. But overall, without the waterfront, it just wasn't camp.

On the hike back from the burying ground we stopped at an IGA to buy candy bars. Ramon jokingly said to the man behind the fish counter, "What? No shark? Figured you'd have plenty in stock." When the man explained that there wasn't any decent sort of edible shark to be had anywhere near Shelter Island, Ramon told him about Tinker's waterfront ban at Quinipet. The fish guy turned to a meat butcher behind another counter.

"You heard anything about sharks in the area?"

"Not a thing," the butcher said. "And my cousin's the harbormaster. If anybody knew, it'd be him, and he'd have told me. It's a small island, word gets around fast."

"Sorry, kids," the fish guy said. "But between him and me, we know all the cops, too, and the fishermen, baymen, and Coast Guardsmen. Somebody's either misinformed you or is pulling your leg."

☾☾☾

Our favorite time was free time, one hour in the afternoon and one hour in the evening to do anything we wanted—*without our counselor*. And without waterfront time on the daily schedule, we squeezed out additional free time.

During those times, Chuck, Spider, Ramon, and I explored every part of the camp, sometimes in pairs, sometimes all four of us together. On Monday we crawled under the girls' cabins and caught snakes and salamanders that we tucked into their bunks while they were out hiking. That evening we walked the road past the Pridwin Hotel until we reached Louis' Beach, where we bought ice cream cones and watched the rich summer kids pay to jump on trampolines.

Since the beachfront of Louis' Beach and the waterfront swimming area of Camp Quinipet were practically adjacent to one another, Chuck decided to ask the man scooping ice cream about the shark sightings. Like the men at the IGA, the scooper hadn't heard a thing about sharks.

"Look out there," he said, pointing to the sandy beach. "Hundreds of people swimming here everyday. Cops ain't said nothing. Coast Guard neither. If we had shark sightings, there'd be signs posted everywhere."

On Tuesday we climbed up the back of the infirmary

roof and rolled small stones from the peak down the front, then scuttered away when the nurse came out to see what the clatter was.

On Wednesday morning we raised the unlocked back window of Croaker's cottage and slipped inside to see what kind of squalor Croaker had lived in. (Maintenance was being handled by someone who lived offsite in Shelter Island Heights.)

The cottage was three rooms and a bath.

"It's pretty empty," Chuck said, testing out a worn recliner that sat in front of a wood stove.

"See if he left a Nazi uniform in the closet," Ramon said, pointing to a door.

Spider opened the closet. Three or four shirts hung alongside two pairs of pants. Two pairs of shoes sat on the floor. There was a green winter jacket on a hook. Spider picked it up and said, "Doesn't look like his infamous Yankees jacket. But he's got plenty of other clothes."

"I thought Dante said Croaker slapped everything in a suitcase and hightailed it out of Dodge," Chuck said.

Ramon began opening and closing dresser drawers. "Tee shirts, underwear, socks, sweaters. Didn't take much with him, I guess."

"The man was on foot," Spider said. "He probably took what he could carry and had to leave a lot behind."

"Must have been in a real hurry," Ramon said.

The camp bell rang for lunch then, and the discussion dead-ended.

☾☾☾

That night we split up for after-supper free time. Ramon and Spider filled up a couple of water balloons and headed across the camp toward the girls' cabins.

Chuck and I followed the main driveway out of

camp, turned left along the main road and followed the shoulder. A minute later we were sitting on a cement wall, looking out over the camp's waterfront. We stared at the bay beyond the famous Quinipet gazebo that had been built on the shorefront rocks. On the far shore we could see the summer cottages' lights twinkling like stars.

"I can't believe Tink the Dink closed the waterfront," I said.

"Hey, get over it," Chuck said. "We can do plenty of swimming once we get back home."

Our families had a wonderful beach directly behind our dairy farm on Long Island Sound. The Sound waters were a little chillier than the bay, but there were more boulders to dive from, and the colder waters were clearer when you opened your eyes underwater.

"Yeah, but there's no war canoe at home," I said glumly.

"Who needs a war canoe? We'll build a raft from beach wood."

"I suppose," I said.

We sat quiet for a while. Chuck broke the silence.

"Hey, why do you suppose the swimming float is out there?"

"What do you mean?" I said. "It's anchored there."

"Yeah, but if there's no swimming, sailing, or canoeing this summer, why's it out?"

"Maybe it's out year-round."

"Nah," Chuck said. "They pull those things out of the water at summer's end so they won't rot, then stash them in the barn for the winter. In early to mid June they drop them back in."

Chuck's father, my Uncle Mo, was the machine shop foreman at Brigham's Shipyard in Greenport. This was the kind of information Chuck soaked up from his father. It made sense.

CROAKER

"But if Tinker declared a shark alert, why would he put the float out at all?" I said. "Why not keep it in storage?"

"Tinker wouldn't have put the float out," Chuck said. "From what you and Dante said about maintenance, it was Croaker's job to do it. Maybe Tinker helped, but Croaker was the handyman."

"But Croaker was already gone a month or so earlier, like back in April or May. Tinker couldn't have done it alone, could he? And why would he?"

"I don't know," Chuck said. "I notice there's no other waterfront equipment out. No picnic tables on the beach. No lifeguard towers. No roped-off swimming area."

In summer at Quinipet you see a huge rectangle of roped-together buoys designating the boundaries of the swimming area. Also inside the roped-off area would be the swimming float.

"Maybe Tinker got the float out there, found it was all too much work to handle with Croaker gone, and stopped right then."

"And so he wouldn't have to finish, he totally made up the shark story," I said. "Which means the guy at the fish counter and the guy at the ice cream counter were right—there are no sharks."

A devilish smile crept over Chuck's face, then over mine. I knew we had the same thought. *War canoes!*

☾☾☾

Chuck and I sat on a log bench outside our cabin as the sun disappeared. We snapped on our flashlights and shone the beams around the grassy area in front of us. Spider and Ramon trotted in from the shadows.

"Hey, you guys," Spider said. "Come with us. You've got to see this."

"See what?" Chuck said.

"Croaker's cabin," Ramon said.

"Seen it before. Remember?" I said.

"But now there's a fire in the woodstove," Spider said.

"With nobody there," Ramon added.

"He's back?" Chuck asked.

"Don't know," Spider said. "We smelled something burning on our way back from the girls' cabins, so we followed our noses. It was smoke from Croaker's chimney. We peeked in and saw the door of the woodstove was open, with a fire in it. But nobody's there."

☾☾☾

"Wait," Spider whispered, putting out a hand as we approached the cottage. "Somebody's there. Hide. In the bushes."

A shadowy figure stood at Croaker's door. It wasn't a big person, so it couldn't be Croaker moving back in. By moonlight we could see the person fumbling with the lock. The door swung open and the firelight from the stove briefly illumined the man's lemon yellow windbreaker. He stepped in and shut the door.

"It's Tinker," Chuck said. "What's he doing here?"

"Shh!" Ramon said. "Let's go see."

With Ramon in the lead, we sneaked forward and hunkered down under the window we had used for our earlier break-in. Ramon eased himself up to the sill and peeked in.

"What's he doing?" Chuck said.

"Looking in the closet," Ramon whispered, ducking back down. "He's got an armful of clothes."

"This is a weird time to be cleaning out Croaker's closet," Chuck said.

Ramon sneaked another peek. "He's stuffing the clothes into the stove."

"We've got to go," Spider said. "The rest of the cabin will be out looking for us."

"One more look," Ramon whispered. Before we could object, he raised his head. "Oops!" he hissed. "I think he saw me. Run."

We lit out like rabbits through the bushes.

☾☾☾

On Thursday morning in the dining hall, as he always did at the start of breakfast, Tinker started off the announcements. Except this morning he was a little red in the face and narrow in the eyes. I knew he meant business. Even though we were indoors, he had on his yellow jacket and the navy blue SUPREME COMMANDER ball cap.

"Apparently several of you campers were out after dark last night and wandered past the caretaker's cabin that used to be Mr. Croaker's residence—until he quit and left." His voice grew sterner. "That is designated as the caretaker's cabin, and it is considered a private residence, just as my house beside it is a private residence. Even though we have no on-site caretaker living in it now, the Board of Directors expects to hire someone for next year. So I'm beginning to clean it out a little bit at a time. Last evening I was disposing of some tattered work uniforms Mr. Croaker left behind. That's when one of you peeked in the window and startled me. Now, I don't care which of you it was. I know kids like to explore. But it's not funny to scare people by sneaking around like that. That caretaker's cottage is off-limits. Stay away from it."

"Tattered work uniforms?" Spider whispered to me as Mr. Tinker continued with other announcements. "He must've been looking in a different closet from the one I saw. Those weren't uniforms."

☾☾☾

That afternoon, after a softball game with Dante's cabin, we had an hour of free time from four until five o'clock. By five-past-four we were crouched behind the boathouse across the road from the waterfront. The camp's fleet of small sailboats, along with their centerboards, masts and sails—anything worth stealing—were locked inside. But under the roof of the lean-to shed attached to the boathouse, upside-down on a wide rack of two-by-fours, lay Quinipet's two war canoes and the outrigger. They weren't chained down or locked inside because, if stolen, they'd be easily identified and recovered.

"Let's see how heavy one is," Ramon said. "Everybody get under and lift."

The canoe was heavy, but the test lift was successful, four of us could manage one. We set the bulky canoe back in place.

"We can't do it now. We'll be seen," Ramon said. "But if we wait until after dark, when the rest of the cabin's asleep, we can sail the seven seas."

"What about Darren?" Chuck said, meaning our counselor.

"He sleeps like the dead," Ramon said. "Every night I hear him snoring like a chainsaw."

"And the sharks?" Spider said, pointing toward the waterfront. "What about Tinker's sharks?" Sometimes Spider could be a little slow on the uptake.

"There's no sharks," I said. "Tinker made it up."

"Besides," Ramon said. "Sharks don't prowl at night. There's no food then. Everybody knows that."

We three stared at Ramon.

"It's true," Ramon said. "It's a known fact."

"Even so," I said, feeling apprehensive about stealing a canoe. "I'm not sure we should—

CROAKER

"Hey, you promised us a ride in a war canoe," Ramon said. "Are we on for tonight or not?" He thrust his right hand into the midst of us and held it there, calling for our Four Musketeers pledge. Spider put his hand on Ramon's, and Chuck laid his hand on theirs.

"Well?" Ramon said.

Reluctantly, I added mine. But something felt wrong. Really wrong.

☾☾☾

It was nine-thirty before everyone else in our cabin settled down and fell asleep. The four of us used an old trick we'd seen in the movies, stuffing pillows and dirty laundry under our blankets to create the illusion of sleeping bodies in the bunks. Then we sneaked out of the cabin with our clothes, shoes, and flashlights and dressed outside.

Fifteen minutes later we were sliding a war canoe into the salt water. The one we chose had the head of an angry dragon at the front.

"Remember, it's dark," I cautioned as we pushed off from the shore. "We don't want to get so far away from the beach that we can't tell where to come back ashore."

"No biggie," Ramon said. "It's an island, remember? We can come in close to shore anywhere and just have to follow close to the coastline. Eventually we'll find the camp."

"Actually," Chuck said, "we've got Quinipet's gazebo for a landmark."

"Not to change the subject," Spider said, "but I don't see any life preservers."

"We're all good swimmers," Ramon said. "Besides, if a tidal wave flipped us over, we'd hang onto the canoe. Right?"

"A tidal wave?" Chuck said.

"Well, that's about the only thing that could tip a canoe this big," Ramon said, standing up and trying to rock the boat side-to-side.

"Hey, knock it off, you moron," Spider said.

Ramon laughed and gave a couple more shakes to show he wasn't stopping just because Spider told him to, then sat back down. "Okay, let's paddle," he said. "Head for that point of land to the right."

We started stroking and the heavy canoe moved forward through the water. The quarter moon hung above the bay, its silver light on the waters creating a path that disappeared in the distance near Greenport. The path beckoned us, invited us, daring us to follow it into deep waters. The only man-made lights on the bay were those of the North Ferry making its scheduled crossings. The view was breathtaking and there was no sound except the paddles dipping in the water. Then, as if on cue, we all stopped on the same stroke and let the heavy canoe coast through the gray waters. It was serene, peaceful, magnificent. We had gotten our ride in a war canoe.

Twenty minutes later we beached the canoe along the swimming area at Louis' Beach. The ice cream stand, snack bar, and trampoline concession had already closed, so no one was around except for a car with steamed-up windows in the parking lot. Ramon and Spider poked around the buildings to see if any food had been left out, and Chuck and I walked the length of the beach.

"Hey, check this out," Chuck said, pointing to a bright yellow beach towel on the sand, a pair of black-framed sunglasses and a dark blue baseball cap on one corner.

"Missing bather, missing bather!" Chuck announced.

"Yeah, one of Tinker's sharks got him," I said.

"No doubt about it," Chuck said. "It's a miracle there aren't more unaccounted-for towels, hats, and sunglasses on this beach. These sharks are a serious problem." He

leaned down and picked up the hat and sunglasses. "Finders, keepers," he said, putting them on.

"You may as well take this, too," I said, snapping the sand from the yellow towel and handing it to him.

"I will," he said, and draped it over his shoulders as if it were a king's mantle. "Losers, weepers."

A voice broke in, Ramon's. "Ready to head back?"

We climbed into the war canoe and shoved off, Chuck in the bow, then me, then Spider, and Ramon paddling in the stern.

"Look," Chuck said, standing up in his new yellow cape and blue ball cap. "I'm George Washington crossing the Delaware." To anyone watching from shore, he probably looked like he was riding the back of the dragon.

"Sit down, General George," Ramon said. "You may be a celebrity on land, but out here everybody rows. Now, mush!"

Chuck sat down and began to paddle. Nobody bothered to correct Ramon's mixed metaphor.

We aimed for the dark point of land to the west where we'd seen the gazebo and put our shoulders into the work. Because of the current, it was slower going in that direction. We made progress, but halfway there we decided to abandon that destination.

"I've seen enough for one night," Spider said. "We can always sneak out again tomorrow night, right? How about we head back in for the waterfront? It'll take a few minutes to get there and put the canoe back on the rack."

"Sounds okay to me," I said. "It's after eleven, and even the Four Musketeers have to sleep a little."

Without argument we turned the dragon's head toward shore and paddled for the camp beach.

"Hey, let's tie up at the float for a minute," Ramon said as we drew near it. "That's another thing we didn't get to check out this week, thanks to Tinker."

We stopped stroking and let our paddles drag in the water until the canoe bumped up against the float sideways.

"Hook a line on, "Ramon commanded as he and Spider stepped up onto the gray platform. It barely dipped in response to their newly added weight, but the war canoe, with me and Chuck still in the front half, popped up in the back half as they stepped free. The front end rode lower in the water by a couple of inches, almost as if something were pulling on the bow. I eased back to the middle of the boat to even out the weight.

"We can't tie on," Chuck said. "There's no rope."

"No rope?" Ramon said. "Well, just hang on, then. We'll only be a minute. Then we'll switch with you."

He and Spider padded back and forth across the gray non-skid decking, trying to get it to rock. Back and forth they ran together until they got a rhythm going. The trapped water and air made slapping sounds as the float rose and fell, small newly created waves rippling away from their source. The canoe bounced on the surface, partly because the ripples buoyed it up, partly because Chuck was holding too tight to the bucking float.

"Aw, come on, you guys," Chuck moaned as he turned in his bow seat to face the center of the canoe. "You're rocking the boat."

But it wasn't just them.

"Watch out!" I shrieked. On the edge of the canoe that had been thudding against the float was a hand—a gigantic, swollen, blanched-white hand. Strands of brown seaweed and stringy green spaghetti grass clung to it, dripping seawater in the moonlight.

"What the—?" Chuck gasped, recoiling in horror, scrambling backward until his back was against the inside of the dragon bow.

I heard the water slosh as a second thick hand clamped onto the edge of the canoe, tipping it even more toward the float now. But being oversized and wide-bottomed, the war canoe wouldn't capsize easily. I gripped my paddle and whacked its blade against the second hand—once, twice, three times.

Chuck yelled, "Hey, you guys, help!" and used his own paddle to beat the first hand, but couldn't throw himself into it because he had to hang onto the float with one arm. The two giant hands from the sea bottom seemed unaffected by our blows, as if they suffered no sense of pain, and refused to let go.

"What's wrong?" Spider asked, and a second later he and Ramon stood gaping over the edge of the float.

"Something's got us!" Chuck screamed. "Help!"

"Get out," Ramon yelled. "Fast. Jump up."

It sounded like a good idea, and Chuck tossed his paddle onto the float. With one arm still anchoring us to the float, he got to his feet on the dragon's back with the yellow towel around his shoulders.

The boat dipped even more to the inside. Something heavy was trying to pull itself up, but there wasn't enough space between canoe and float. The back of the boat started drifting away from the float, as if a wedge was coming up through the gap. I stretched my paddle to Spider and he gripped its blade.

"Hang on, Spider," I said. "We can't leave the canoe. We have to keep it tight against the float or the thing will come up between us. I think it's trapped under the float."

"This has got to be a joke, right?" Ramon said. Then he yelled down through the cracks in the gray decking of the float, "Okay, joke's over. Come out, come out, whoever you are!"

Suddenly the thick blanched hands released their grip and slipped below the surface. The canoe buoyed and leveled. Chuck seized the moment and jumped ship, landing on the gray decking. He walked to the far corner of the float, leaving Spider and me, connected by my paddle, to keep the canoe from drifting away.

"Where'd it go?" Spider said. "And what was it?"

"I don't know," Ramon answered. "But it's time to—"

Before he could finish, the two hands broke the surface and clamped onto the canoe again, this time to the outside edge, close to the dragon's back where Chuck had been standing. The bow of the canoe dipped as whatever was below tried to draw up its waterlogged weight.

What looked like a jellyfish appeared on the surface,

a swirl of drifting tendrils that emanated from a round gelatinous center. But when the tendrils caught the moonlight, the strands turned blond. This wasn't a jellyfish, it was the top of a head, a swollen grayish head with bloated, rotting skin. It broke the surface slowly, the way an alligator does, eyes suddenly blinking on the waters of a muddy swamp. But this was no alligator; it didn't blink, and its sockets held no eyes.

Yet it looked. It looked at the bow of the canoe, as if it had seen something there that wasn't there any more. Something—some sort of fabric—floated back from where shoulders must have once been under its neck and head. The fabric was blue, like a cape—no, a jacket, a dark blue jacket, with a bright white emblem on it—a New York Yankees emblem! It was Croaker! I was sure of it. Had something happened when he was anchoring the float? But this wasn't just a drowned body, a floater popped to the surface, freed from under the swimming float by Ramon and Spider's shaking. This thing, whatever it was, was dead, but not fully dead. It had gripped the boat. Twice. And here it was again, surfacing, seeking. Croaker wasn't fully dead.

The head moved awkwardly from side to side like a mime, like a robot scanning a scene, its lower jaw moving as the hole that had once been its mouth opened and closed mutely. There was something sad about it, and terrifying at the same time. Then the swollen hands let go their grip, the canoe bobbed back to level, and the bloated head and drifting blond hair disappeared beneath the surface again, the blue jacket trailing behind as it sank into the depths.

I let my breath out and tried to breathe regularly again. I hadn't realized I'd been holding it.

"Where'd it go this time?" Ramon gasped out, staring at Spider and me as we clung to the ends of the canoe paddle.

Before we could answer, Chuck yelled, "There it is!"

I stood up in the canoe and all three of us stared at Chuck on the far corner of the float, pointing at the water in front of him. Croaker's head showed above the surface, the lower half of his empty eye sockets filled with seawater, the upper half of them cupping the night air. We four stood as if we'd been turned to stone. The memory of an alligator came into my mind again, and I suddenly realized why.

"Chuck, he's moving!" I shouted. "He's coming for you!"

Croaker glided faster in the water, as if forced to quicken his attack in the face of my warning. My cousin stood transfixed like someone watching an accident happening.

"Chuck!" I screamed. "Get back!"

Chuck's head snapped my way. He'd heard me, and he took a quick step away from the edge of the float.

Thwack! Croaker's thick right hand smacked the gray decking, then his left. He pulled his heavy body right up to the float and stretched an arm forward, trying to reach Chuck's ankle. Chuck backed up another step. The float sagged and dipped toward Croaker, and I could see that he was straining to pull his waterlogged body onto the float. A deep throaty growl like that of a prowling lion came from deep down inside him. But this wasn't about hunger. This was about revenge.

And that's when I suddenly saw Chuck the way Croaker must have seen him.

"Take off the towel, Chuck!" I screamed.

Croaker thrust his other arm onto the float and began lifting himself on his forearms, working to get his chest up. Chuck stood frozen in terror.

"And the hat!" I yelled. "Take off the hat!"

The blue hat didn't say SUPREME COMMANDER,

but blue was blue, and coupled with the yellow towel that could be mistaken for a lemon-yellow windbreaker, I was sure I knew what it wanted. "It thinks you're Tinker. Croaker thinks you're Tinker."

The thing pulled its torso onto the float, struggling to get a first leg aboard. The side of its head that I could see appeared to be crushed like an eggshell. A few strands of blond hair from the top of the head disappeared into the shattered side of the skull. It reached out for Chuck's ankle then, as if it was unsure whether to grab its prey first or finish getting the leg onto the float. But it seemed determined that nothing would deter it from its mission.

Chuck yanked off the hat and dropped it in front of what had been Croaker's face, then stripped the yellow towel from his shoulders and draped it over what was left of the caretaker's head. Maybe it would blind him.

"Let's go!" I cried. "Now!"

The others leaped into the war canoe and I pushed off from the swimming float. We paddled for land like madmen, never speaking, never looking back, and sprang ashore the instant the dragon nosed up onto the sandy beach. It was only then that we looked back, first at the waters behind the boat to see if the thing was slogging ashore, then back at the float. The thing stood in the center of it, outlined in the moonlight, the hat in one hand, the towel in the other, lifting its fists heavenward like some frustrated Frankenstein monster. It was terrifying and yet pathetic, seeing the remains of Croaker standing there on that float. I felt strangely sorry, sad.

We ran to the cabin and woke Darren, our counselor, quickly spilling out our story. He was skeptical, but nevertheless, our pleading convinced him to follow us to the waterfront.

The war canoe was exactly where we had beached it. The float was empty. No person stood or sat or lay on it. No sign of the towel or the blue hat, at least not from that distance. And Darren wasn't about the paddle out there to check. Nor were we.

"Let's put the canoe and paddles back on the rack," he said patiently. "Then it's back to bed. I know you were bored without waterfront this week, so I won't tell your parents about this." Despite our protests, Darren hushed us and made us promise to go to sleep.

We couldn't let it go, though. It had really happened. It had almost gotten us killed. Croaker hadn't quit and left, he was dead, perhaps from an accident, perhaps murdered. We four knew we had a bunch of pieces to the puzzle, but we didn't know how to fit them together. One thing was sure: we couldn't go to Tinker.

So the next morning we went to Mrs. Wesley, the woman who taught arts-and-crafts. Her other job was to produce the camp newspaper each Saturday, publishing stories about the week's campers and camping experiences, so everyone would have a keepsake to take home. She was the only investigative type we knew, and she listened intently.

But then, while we were at lunch, she ratted us out. She told Tinker himself, who called us on the carpet. He insisted we tell it all again. We told him. Oddly, he seemed more worried than angry, and he let us go without scolding or punishing us. That was Friday.

On Saturday morning we woke to a light drizzle. After breakfast two hundred of us campers packed our gear, cleaned up our cabins, and piled into the meeting hall for the goodbye ceremony. Mr. Tinker had always led it, then gave each counselor a chance to speak.

But Mr. Tinker didn't show. After waiting a half hour, the counselors took over and finished up the formalities. Another hour passed. The buses failed to show up. Mrs. Wesley sent people out to search for Tinker. The nurse phoned the North Ferry to see what the holdup was.

Kids began calling home to say they'd be late, that something was wrong.

"The North Ferries aren't operating," the nurse announced. "They've been shut down due to an emergency. Your buses have been rerouted to the South Side and will be coming to Shelter Island by way of the South Ferry. Everything will be four to five hours later than originally announced. Although it wasn't on your original schedule, the camp will provide lunch. We're sorry for the inconvenience."

It was suppertime before we got home to Greenport. The North Ferries never did run that night, and because we had to depart Shelter Island by the South Ferry to Long Island's South Fork, it meant driving seventy-five extra miles.

The next day's *Newsday* ran a front page story saying the North Ferry had been shut down from Friday night through Sunday morning. Not one of the three ferries had been allowed to cross the bay and use the Shelter Island slip. A photo showed the terminal, the wooden pilings, the bulkheads, all roped off with Crime Scene tape. Divers spent two days searching the area. The *Newsday* reporter had persuaded the ferry's purser to make the same statement he'd made to police.

"On the 5:30 boat we had eight cars. The fellow in the very front got out of his car—a lemon yellow Volkswagen beetle that matched his jacket—and leaned on the front gate. I told him not to lean on the gate. I remember him because he wore his hair in a hippy ponytail that stuck through the back of his ball cap. I joked about what it said: SUPREME COMMANDER. But he wasn't in a joking mood. He was the nervous type and tried to light a cigarette, so I reminded him it was no smoking. Then he leaned on the front gate again, and I had to warn him not to lean on it or on the side of the boat, that it was dangerous. It's posted on the signs. I turned away from him for a second to collect from another driver. Then I turned back to tell him he could smoke INSIDE his car. And just as I turn to tell him, I see somebody, or something, dripping wet and covered in seaweed, climb in over the railing—from the water side onto the car deck—and it wraps its arms around the guy, pinning his arms to his sides. Then it—this big thing—picks him up and they tumble over the side together—splash! By the time I get to the spot, they're both gone."

The article continued on to say that divers spent all night and much of the next morning searching for the missing persons. The ferry boats had to be shut down because of the prop wash, and even after the bodies were found, the area needed to be checked for weapons and other evidence.

Although no names were released pending notification of kin, it was thought that the first victim, found wearing a New York Yankees jacket, was Camp Quinipet's caretaker. His body had apparently been submerged for months. The second victim was presumed to be the Camp Manager, who was seen at work on Friday morning and whose driverless car was aboard the ferry. Divers had to bring both bodies up at the same time, because they were inseparable. They found the two entangled in seaweed, with the arms and legs of the bloated caretaker wrapped around the one in the lemon yellow windbreaker. The blue ball cap saying SUPREME COMMANDER was found jammed in the camp manager's mouth.

The Cave

BUTTERFLIES? BUTTERFLIES! The cave was filled with butterflies, hundreds, thousands of them. Tom Shire had never seen anything like it. In all his years of spelunking—exploring caves, collecting rocks, minerals, pieces of ore—he'd never seen such a thing. Imagine! A cave filled with butterflies.

The cave was thick with them. They weren't just hanging on the walls. They fluttered around, filling the air, covering the floor, creating a cloud around Tom's head. He kept his mouth closed and breathed through his nose. Only the light from his headlamp and flashlight held them at bay. When he walked across the cave it was like parting a curtain, the creatures dividing where his headlamp and flashlight shone, so he wasn't sure if it was because of the light or the heat.

The cave wasn't totally dark. Around the edges it was dark and shadowy, yes, where the walls and floor met. But the center of the room was brighter, a column of natural light streaming down a large natural funnel in the cave's roof. This cavern he'd climbed up into, this almost perfectly circular room, reminded him of a giant free-standing Scandinavian fireplace. *A chimney rock,* the Indians would have called it in earlier times. So long as the sun was high in the overhead sky, the chimney let some light in.

Tom gauged the height from the floor to the lowest part of the chimney hole to be twelve to fifteen feet. The throat of the chimney extended another six or eight feet to the earth's surface. The room's curved walls reminded him of a geodesic dome. He guessed it to be a hundred feet across.

But it didn't make sense, butterflies congregating in a cave. They'd be drawn to the light, wouldn't they—or was that moths? And didn't butterflies need the leaves and vegetation outside for a food source? Yet here they were, thousands of them—maybe tens of thousands—living inside this cave. How could it be? What did it mean? Why didn't they flutter up the chimney to the warm air and sunshine?

Tom's headlamp caught a rainbow of colors, the full spectrum, the predominant ones being black and orange. *Monarchs*, he thought, which made sense. They were the most common species of butterfly in this region. Butterflies weren't his specialty, but the monarchs he was sure about. Just the idea that he recognized one of the many types comforted him.

There was no wildlife in the cave, not that he could see. No bears, thank God, but then again this wasn't hibernation season, nor was there any apparent way for them to get in or out. He expected a few bats, considering the perfect entrance and exit the chimney offered, but when he probed the ceiling with his flashlight, he saw no sign of any.

Tom snapped off his headlamp to save it, and used just the flashlight to examine the overhead. How perfectly rounded the cave roof was, how smooth. *Limestone*, he thought, judging by its color, which would make sense for this area.

He shone the light on the floor. As he had suspected from the roughness and striations underfoot: *granite*. One look confirmed it. But that didn't make sense. Why would the cave's floor be granite and its dome limestone? He pictured his wife's cheese server, essentially a wooden cutting board with a glass cover.

The two materials didn't necessarily have to be the same, did they?

Tom sat perfectly still on the rough floor trying to count the different kinds of butterflies. He wasn't actually sure about species, but he could differentiate colors and patterns. By the time he reached ten, though, many more landed on his hands and arms, and in no time he was covered with them. *They have weight*, he thought. Individually it wasn't so noticeable, but there was a cumulative effect. He shook them off and shone his flashlight up again. *They have barely enough airspace to hover.* The cramped creatures had to be beating against each other with their wings.

He aimed the light at the floor, and hundreds of butterflies lifted off. Others that had been hovering above them immediately took their place. *They're taking turns, flying in shifts, resting in shifts. There's cooperation here. They're working together.*

Tom snapped off his light and relit the headlamp. He wanted to examine the area where the floor and walls met—something felt odd about it, wrong. That meant crawling on hands and knees toward the dark corners, away from the natural light, where the ceiling curved lower. He started forward through a cloud of beating wings, feeling as much as seeing his way.

His right hand struck something, knocking it forward. *Something about it sounded familiar, something about the way it scraped the granite floor.* He moved his hand forward slowly and felt around until his fingers grazed it. *A headlamp*. With his free hand he dusted a cloud of butterflies out of his face and focused his own headlamp on it. *Identical to his own*. Someone had left it behind. But who would do that? No cave explorer he knew. He clicked it on, but it was dead.

Tom edged forward again. His hand grazed something else. He felt it, not even having to shine his

headlamp on it this time. *Another headlamp.* Dead. Beside it lay a flashlight, also dead.

Tom got to his feet and, even with his headlamp on, snapped on his flashlight, hoping more light would dispel the fear gnawing at his gut. He swatted his way through the cloud of butterflies, keeping the flashlight beam aimed at the floor ahead. *Headlamps, flashlights, and fanny packs.* Caving gear lay scattered everywhere.

He stopped. Something was wrong. *Why had so many cavers visited the domed chamber only to leave their equipment behind?* Was it a shrine? Was it like visitors leaving pictures and flowers and personal items at the foot of The Wall, the Vietnam Memorial in Washington, D.C.? He recalled the names of a half dozen missing cave explorers he'd read or heard about over the years: Ray Jackson, Henri Toulouse and Martha Jameson, Frank and Barry Montgomery, and, of course, his own brother Hal, whose disappearance was one of the reasons he'd come exploring here. A shiver ran through his body. *Hal?*

Tom turned back toward the shaft of sunlight streaming down from the chimney. Had the hole he'd come up through been under the spotlight or was it just outside it? Something told him it was time to leave, and the hole he'd come in by might be his only way out. It was near the center of the cave, he was sure of that, and it was only slightly wider than his shoulders. It had been a tight squeeze. He had to find the hole.

But the question nagged at Tom: *limestone walls and a granite floor?* He needed to check the joint where the wall and floor came together. Turning back toward the outer darkness, he waded through even more caving gear until his head almost banged into the wall. Then he knelt down and leaned forward into the tight V. *Something odd here.* He unhooked the rock hammer from his belt and tapped the wall, expecting a chink-chink sound. But it

wasn't. He rapped in several more places, high and low, and to the right and the left. Same sound—*metallic*. He smacked as hard as he could, but couldn't break through, the sound reminding him of banging a wrench on a thousand-gallon fuel tank at his uncle's house. *The walls were cast iron or steel or some alloy. They'd been made to look like limestone.*

Tom shone the flashlight where the wall met the granite floor. The floor was notched, channeled. It had a groove all the way around, and the metal wall had been fitted precisely into the groove. He crab-walked sideways to the left, checking the seal as he went, hoping for a break, or an imperfection, or a hatch door, even a manufacturer's logo or part number, who knew what might be there? But it was engineered perfectly. *Did it have an O-ring seal, too? What was going on here?*

When Tom was sure he'd gone full circle, he stopped, then backed up toward the center of the cave again, toward the light. He gazed up at the chimney. The sky was clouding over. His watch said it was 2:10. Even though it wouldn't be dark outside for a few hours, the cave was losing the light as the sun sank. He needed to get out.

A low, slow, grating sound came from floor level to his right. *Like a cement block being dragged over another cement block*. It was moving rock. *The hole was closing!*

Tom scanned the floor but he saw no hole, only solid granite. The cloud of butterflies felt thicker, denser, as if they were purposely blocking his vision. He flailed away at them and searched the floor, trying to fight the sense of panic rising inside him.

He decided to try a grid search to be sure he didn't miss a spot. He set the flashlight on the floor at the edge of the sunlit oval then backed away until he was at the oval's far edge, removing his headlamp so he could mark that spot, too, its beam upward. Using the line between the two lights as his compass, Tom paced back and forth like a plowman harrowing a field. *No hole.*

He widened the grid search beyond the oval. *Still nothing.* The hole wasn't within the sunlight circle, nor was it around the outer edges of it. He struggled to catch a deep breath, but his chest felt the way it had when he'd had allergies as a child. He tried to tell himself to relax. He could make it awhile with shallow breaths. *Save your strength while you figure out what to do next. Don't give in to the fear.*

Tom sat down to relax and think. *Had the hole moved?* No. The grating sound could have been the hole closing, of course, though he preferred to not believe that, for it would add to his—*don't mention fear.* Besides, he hadn't seen any slab that had slid across to cover a hole—at least not within the bounds of the sunlit oval. Then it struck him: *the hole hadn't moved, the sunlit area had. It had been a circle when he entered the cave, an oval now. Of course, as the sun shifted across the sky, the lighted area changed.* But had the previously lighted area—if that was where the hole was—had it been beyond the flashlight or the headlamp he'd used as markers? How far beyond?

Tom glanced up the chimney shaft. The sun moved from east to west, from low in the sky to directly overhead at noon, to low in the sky on the opposite side later. Which meant the spotlight effect when he'd entered the cave must have been farther to the right than the current area. He stretched his arms and began searching farther to the right beyond the lighted oval. Two sweeps, three, four. *Nothing.* He tried not to think about the grating sound. *It was him against the cave, wasn't it?* To think it might be him against the cave and something else—something more intentionally insidious—that was too much to bear.

He looked up the chimney again. Something wasn't right about it. He felt around for a rock, but there was none to be found, nothing but caving gear. *But this was a cave, and surely there must be loose stones somewhere.* He gripped his hammer, wound up like a softball pitcher and let it fly underhand as hard as he could. It went straight up the center of the chimney—*thunk*—and fell back down, striking the floor close by. *What in blazes had it hit—a plexiglass ceiling, a thick glass window, a force field?* Or was it his imagination?

No wonder the butterflies hadn't left. They couldn't. They were imprisoned in a huge sealed terrarium.

His chest felt tight again, his breaths shallower and more labored. He sat down and crossed his legs in a lotus position, wrists over thighs so he could practice the yoga relaxation technique he'd learned. *Deep breath in through the nose, hold it, exhale through the mouth.* He felt butterflies on his bare upturned palms, his shoulders, all over. He didn't bother to retrieve the still-lit headlamp or the flashlight. The relaxation technique was what mattered now.

Tom's hair grew damp and sweaty, and butterflies landed on it, their fluttering wings tickling his ears. One landed on his nose, but he kept his eyes shut and didn't attempt to brush it away. A few more touched down on his cheeks and forehead, on his eyelashes and eyelids, on the dimples beside his mouth, on his lips. They didn't feel threatening; they were simply there, wanting to alight, to rest, as he wanted to rest.

Even with his eyes closed, Tom could feel more butterflies landing on top of the first layer covering his body, and a moment later another layer on top of that, a thickening blanket of butterflies. He concentrated on relaxing, breathing in through his nose and out through his mouth, his thoughts no longer about escape or rescue, only about relaxing.

He heard a hiss, the finest, quietest hiss he'd ever heard, like gas escaping. But it wasn't gas, at least not from some outside source. This was right next to his ears.

He relaxed more deeply—*I'm going numb*—as the sheer weight of them—*it's the butterflies hissing*—forced him onto his back on the dark floor. *This feels like Hal pinning me under the mattress. Relax. In through the nose, out through the mouth.* He heard a delicate flutter, thousands of wings—*fanning, cooling*—and the hiss again, ever so fine—*anesthetic*—and then their tiny nicking, clicking teeth, first on his ears and his nose, and then, when he was screaming and his mouth was filling with them, on the papery film of his eyelids and his tongue.

Night Train to Plantation 13

I KEPT MY EYES AVERTED, not wanting to meet the UPS driver's gaze as I signed for the two packages from Maine. He couldn't have missed the return addresses, a funeral home on one, Augusta Mental Health Institute on the other. Light bulbs had to be flashing on in his head. I figured he'd recognize the heavy, smaller box as cremation ashes, an item he'd no doubt delivered before. Not every UPS package required a signature, but a box containing a person's remains, even if only ashes, would surely require a signature, probably for legal issues.

The other parcel, the one from AMHI, apparently required a signature for a different reason. It wasn't because it exceeded any particular dollar value—I had an idea what was inside and doubted the contents were worth a total of fifty dollars—but likely required delivery acknowledgment for the sender. *Official Business*, AMHI had stamped it. And, as if those two words and the return address being a State Hospital weren't accusing enough, a social worker had penned on it in red ink: *YOUR FATHER'S EFFECTS*. I was sure I felt the driver's eyes burning into me as I scrawled my signature on the electronic clipboard. I felt embarrassed and ashamed.

Back in the security of my apartment I sat on the couch and stared at the packages. The smaller, heavier box from the mortuary seemed less threatening, so I slit it open with my house key. An unsealed envelope lay on top with *ATTN: Arnold Burnett* typed on it. I opened it and slid out a funeral director's card that identified the ashes as my father's. It also listed a few vital statistics. Name: Robert Burnett. Age at death: 42, which I had known. Place and date of death: Augusta, Maine, which I had known. Marital status: never married, which I had known. Place and date of birth: Plantation 13, Maine, which I had not known. My father had never spoken of his hometown except to mention Bangor, Maine, where he had spent his early years with his own father.

Beneath the cards sat a thick-walled plastic bag that reminded me of the potting soil I had bought in Wal-Mart, its top puckered and tied off like a belly button. The bag filled the inside of the box completely the way milk spreads to occupy the shape of a milk carton. I opened the top of the bag and touched the ashes, feeling the softness and the grittiness between my thumb and fingers, and letting it sift through. I recalled a line from a soap opera's opening credits: *like sands through the hourglass,* then dug my thumb and fingers deeper into the ashes as if I were clamming a beach below the low water line. My middle fingertip met something hard, a tiny foreign object that wasn't ashes, and when I worked it free I realized it was a tiny fragment of bone that hadn't been totally incinerated. I felt around and discovered more bits of grit and gristle. I had read that this was common, but this was first-hand and it unnerved me to be sitting on my couch with my father's remains on my fingers and under my fingernails and in the wrinkles of my knuckles. I set the ashes box on an end table and went to wash my hands in the kitchen. My father wasn't going anywhere. I could handle the disposition of the ashes later.

When I got back to the couch, I opened the AMHI box and spread its contents—my deceased father's officially itemized personal effects—on the coffee table. There wasn't much: the clothing he'd been wearing when they checked him in—a pair of black socks, a pair of tan work boots without laces (no doubt removed for his

safety), white underpants and white tee shirt, a pair of Lee blue jeans (38W x 34L), a blue chamois work shirt (Large), a worn black belt (probably taken from him when he was institutionalized, then returned to me after his death, unlike the disappeared shoe laces), a pair of soft brown work gloves, a hand-knit green-and-white ski cap. In a clear plastic bag I found a promotional pen from the Portland Savings Bank, a dime and three pennies, a Swiss Army knife, and an apartment key. Another plastic bag contained a worn leather wallet shaped by my father's buttock, a ten and three singles. Thirteen cents in change and thirteen bucks in bills. What a lucky guy.

Inside the wallet, a plastic photo insert held his driver's license, social security card, and a snapshot of me in his arms at age three. Even then it had been obvious that I was his kid. We had the same wild hair, flaming red, the same freckled faces, and the same broad, toothy grins.

Another similarity was our eyes. His left eye—which was a glass eye—was a mesmerizing green, an almost perfect match for his right eye, which was a match for *my* right eye. But the similarity ended there, because although he had a glass left eye, I had no left eye, none at all. What people saw when they looked at me—until the year I turned five and started wearing a black eye patch—was flesh, a sealed eyelid that they mistook for a gigantic skin graft. I had no left eye and, thankfully, no open left socket. This drew unwanted attention, countless intrusive questions, and caused me great embarrassment. People asked why the lid had been sewn shut, and my father would explain that it wasn't stitched but was a congenital defect—the skin had always been that way, there was no functional eye behind the lid, no optic nerve, and corrective surgery would not restore my sight.

When I set my father's wallet back on the coffee table, I caught myself rubbing the eyelid hidden behind the patch. I felt something stir inside me. At twenty-one years old, for the first time in my life, I experienced something I had never felt in my teenage years—a deep yearning to be with someone of the opposite sex. I sat a few minutes trying to make sense of it. This was new to me, yet I found I was clear about what the feeling was, though not about what it meant or how to respond to it.

The last item on the table was a purple velvet bag with black drawstrings, a poke bag like a prospector might use for gold dust or a school kid for marbles. The bag hadn't been mine, but I felt it trying to trigger a memory. I'd seen it before, but where? Someone had pulled its strings tight and pinched a sticky label around the top to seal it. I fingered the label, smoothed it out, and made out my father's handwriting: *For Arnie.* I squeezed the bag like it was a Christmas present whose contents I was trying to guess. A marble, a big one. And something papery, maybe a letter. I sat back on the couch, heart fluttering, hands trembling.

I had seen my father only once in the last two years, and that was after AMHI had the Maine and Connecticut State Police track me down to say he was in the State Hospital. He'd had a breakdown. His diagnosis was bipolar disorder along with adult-onset schizophrenia, and the prognosis sounded bleak. I was devastated.

The one time I visited him he was withdrawn, noncommunicative, fragile—shattered. When I saw him curled up on a mattress on the floor of his room, I could hardly bear it. Trite as it may sound, the phrase *a shadow of his former self* perfectly described the man I saw that day. I was confused and ashamed, and in my weakness and isolation I cut him out of my life, exorcised him. I left my father stranded in the mental ward. With absolutely no relatives and very few friends, it was all I could do to take care of myself.

But although I had deserted him, he hadn't abandoned me. Here he was in my living room.

I ripped off the gummy label and loosened the mouth of the bag, half expecting steam or smoke to spew out and a genie to appear. Then, heart on tiptoes, I tipped the bag and the huge round object slid out the bag's throat and plopped against my palm. I stared at it, then started to giggle, and to laugh, and a minute later I was crying and laughing at the same time. There, staring up from my palm lay not a marble but my father's green glass eye. I hadn't recognized the bag at first, because he used it only once in a blue moon for storage, like the week he was fighting an infection of the socket and

couldn't wear it. Most often the bag sat in the drawer of his bedside table.

"Someday it'll be yours," he'd said a couple of times when I was young, but he never explained.

I'd always wondered why I might want it, since I had no socket in which to place it. Why would he pass it on to me? But here it was, my bizarre inheritance.

I lifted my eye patch and held the glass eye against the web of flesh, imagining myself inserting it into an empty socket the way my high school friends had popped in their contacts. Would I then look as normal as my father had? I walked to the bathroom and gazed into the mirror. The green eye was an almost perfect match for my good eye, and for a moment I fantasized gouging out a socket with a teaspoon so I could force it in.

A wave of melancholy washed over me—was that it, melancholy? For the days when I'd been young and my father had been alive and active in my growing up? Or was it sadness and grief at losing him, at feeling lost now without him, at suddenly being an orphan?

As I rolled the glass eye around with my thumb, it struck me that it was neither. The feeling wasn't nostalgia or even grief. It was more like homesickness, but it wasn't about yearning for a place I'd been before; this was an instinctual pull toward someplace I'd *never* been, this was a primal feeling like birds get when it's time to migrate.

I set the eye on my father's folded white tee shirt on the coffee table, picked up the purple bag again, and drew out a folded piece of paper. It was a letter from my father dated two years earlier, two nights before he was committed to AMHI.

Dearest Arnie, my son,

Please forgive me for disappearing last month, but I had no choice. I prayed the breakdown and the

mental disintegration would never come for me, but I knew in my heart it would. I even knew when. My cycle is just like my own father's, 42/21, and his father's, and his father's father's. No doubt it's yours, too. Our family line pays a terrible price to continue, always hoping things will be different, better, less cruel for the next generation. So far, though, nothing has changed.

I cannot explain what may lie ahead for you. If you follow my footsteps and my father's and his father's, it will be both an adventure and a curse. I will not tell you what to do or not do, just as my father did not tell me. We make our own choices. I can only tell you this, if you resist the deep yearning awakening in you now, you may live to old age. If you feel you cannot, if you do as I did, you'll find incredible joy, but only for a short while. I have always loved you, my son, and I have never regretted my own choice.

Your loving father,
Robert Burnett

Paper-clipped to the bottom of the letter was an old punched train ticket from Maine. Passage was from Bangor to Eagle Lake to Plantation 13 and back. The ticket had been used twenty-one years earlier, on the day I was born.

☾☾☾

Two weeks later, during my college's weeklong break, I boarded a bus in New Haven and headed for Maine. Since my father's ashes and letter had arrived and I'd held his glass eye against my eyelid, I had found it impossible to concentrate on class work. My heart ached. At twenty-one I was finally feeling like a lovesick teenager.

Throughout my teens I had been, for all practical purposes, asexual. Neither males nor females had turned me on. I simply had no interest. But now I *yearned*, I felt desire. But although my eyes wandered after women, it wasn't for just any women, it was women pushing strollers and carriages and carrying their infants in slings across their bellies. It took me awhile to clarify it, but I soon saw that it wasn't the women I wanted, it was the babies I coveted. I was like a middle-aged woman whose biological clock was ticking too loudly. Not having a child led me to unexpected fits of weeping that caught me off guard. They crept up and blindsided me, and often I sat sobbing at the preciousness and beauty of life, marveling at the miracle of one generation being able to pass itself along to another. Something deep, something primal, was drawing me to northern Maine to my father's home of origin. And though I had never been given a birth certificate, I was sure sure that his home of origin was also mine.

That afternoon around 1:30 I found myself in the Greyhound station in Bangor, asking where the railway station was so I might catch a train north.

"Ain't no passenger trains out of Bangor, not for years, just freights," the aged ticket agent said through the grillwork of his cubicle. "If you're going north to Millinocket, Houlton, Fort Kent nowadays, you drive or take the bus."

"What about Plantation 13?" I asked.

"Plantation 13?" he said, a note of incredulity in his voice. Then he turned on his stool and called to the fat man sitting behind him at an office desk, "Hey, Charlie, a second one for Plantation 13."

Charlie the manager creaked back heavily in his swivel chair, rose, and edged in beside the older man at the ticket window.

"Okay, here's the deal," he said. "I'll tell you the same thing I told the other young man."

I pulled off my ski cap then, and my hair caught the two men's attention, momentarily diverting the conversation.

"You two brothers?" Charlie said, furrowing his brow.

I shook my head. "Don't know any others. Why?"

"You're both redheads," he said. "And same black eye patch."

"And the other kid is going to Plantation 13, too," the old ticket agent added. "He came in last night, must have taken a hotel. His bus leaves in half an hour."

"Bus for where?" I said.

"It's the Houlton run, but the driver'll drop the kid off at Eagle Lake. They still run an old log train from there out to Plantation 13."

"So Plantation 13 is a town?" I asked.

"Well, yes and no," Charlie said. "You see, a plantation is a sizeable geographical area with no formal government. The land is largely uninhabited, usually cared for by the big paper companies that contract to log them. The only people that far out in the boondocks work in the logging operations."

"What you refer to as Plantation 13," the ticket agent interrupted, "is no more than a cluster of shacks that threatened to blossom into a village shortly after World War II. But it didn't work out. It was too far off the beaten path to support gas stations and supermarkets. What's there now is little more than a ghost town for fifty or a hundred die-hards who are too stubborn to leave."

"Definitely no hospital, right?" I said.

"Houlton would be the closest," Charlie said. "Why do you ask that?"

"I was wondering where babies would be born."

"Home, I expect," he said. "Unless they plan ahead

and stay with friends or relatives in Houlton about the time they're due."

My father's birthplace hadn't been listed as Houlton. The card had read Plantation 13.

"Will I have to piggyback a ride on a log car?"

"No," Charlie said. "The log train has an engine, a coal car, one or two log flatcars, and a caboose. You and the other kid will end up riding in the caboose with the conductor. It's not heated, but it's out of the wind."

"How come there's no passenger car?" I asked.

"Because," said the ticket agent, that train has two purposes: to get supplies from Eagle Lake to Plantation 13, and to haul logs from Plantation 13 to Eagle Lake. Strictly speaking, it's not supposed to carry passengers."

"But I can get a ticket, right?"

"At the café in Eagle Lake they'll sell you a ticket," Charlie said. "But it's a wink-wink sort of thing, not strictly legal. So the waitress will give you one of the old train tickets they sold twenty-five years ago. Just buy it and give it to the old conductor and he'll let you ride in the caboose with him."

"So when does it run? Tonight or tomorrow?"

"It only runs the first and fifteenth, and today's the fifteenth," the ticket agent said. "It's an odd arrangement that has them run two trips today. The locomotive, coal car, and caboose belong to Eagle Lake, but the log cars are the lumber company's and stay in Plantation 13 so they can load them. They leave Eagle Lake and haul supplies to Plantation 13 in the morning, hook up to the log cars, bring them back to Eagle Lake, then make a second trip back so they can return the log cars, and then run empty back to Eagle Lake."

"So the train's already gone today?" I said, alarmed.

"On the supply run, yes, and to bring back the logs," Charlie said. "But after supper they'll leave Eagle Lake on the second run and come back at midnight."

"So I have to go to Plantation 13 and ride back the same night?" I said, wondering how I could track down any relatives or get any information in a couple of hours.

"Yep," the ticket agent said. "Unless you want to stay two weeks. Your ticket'll be punched anyway, so it's up to you. You don't have to decide beforehand."

"So it's a couple of hours or two weeks?"

The two men nodded.

"Is there a hotel?"

The two men shrugged and Charlie said, "We're not travel agents. All we can do is sell you a bus ticket to Eagle Lake."

"You in? We've already phoned to say the other kid is coming," the ticket agent said.

I bought a ticket and as I walked away I heard the ticket agent say to Charlie the manager, "Happens every year around this time, doesn't it? Like the swallows returning to Capistrano."

☾☾☾

On the bus trip to Eagle Lake I sat with the other redhead. Tim was from upstate New York, stood four inches taller than I, and spoke in a deeper voice. He also had ruddier skin and more freckles. Except for our height, weight, and skin tone, we had a lot in common. Our unmanageable, flame-red hair looked like we'd both dyed it from the same bottle and our green right eyes matched perfectly. We were twenty-one, born the same day, just as our fathers had been born the same day and died at age forty-two the same day in separate mental institutions. Neither Tim nor I had known our mothers nor ever thought to ask about them. Under our eye patches we had the same congenital defect, the sealed eyelid.

In talking we discovered we were both loners, not because we *chose* to be, but because we felt a *natural* separateness from other human beings and didn't feel a strong attraction to anyone, either male or female. But we had both found a deep primordial longing, a magnetic attraction toward our roots that seemed to have awakened in us right after the deaths of our fathers. We were like moths drawn to a flame, and I doubt either of us could have abandoned the quest. Something was pulling us, something stronger even than the need to discover our history and origin. We were experiencing feelings so intense that we couldn't begin to fathom them.

We also had in common our fathers' glass eyes. Tim's lay nestled in a hard plastic jewelry case that had been made for a ring. He kept it in his breast pocket close to his heart. Mine lay warm and secure in its purple bag in my side pocket, the bag's drawstrings tied to my belt.

☾☾☾

"We get the train tickets for Plantation 13 inside, right?" Tim asked the driver after we clambered down the bus steps at the Eagle Lake Café.

The driver shrugged, the door shut, and the bus chugged away.

"Better get inside and grab a hamburger, boys," said a voice behind us. "Train leaves in fifteen minutes."

We turned and saw a man leaning out the café's front door. Judging by his furrowed face, he was well past retirement, but still he wore the black uniform and hard-billed hat of a railroad conductor. Protruding from under his hat was a thinning layer of not gray but flaming red hair. I could see by the light of the porch bulb that he wore a black patch over his eye. When he caught us staring at it, he flipped the patch up and revealed a fleshy eyelid sealed like mine.

"Food and tickets in the café," he said, and walked inside.

The café was warm and its only waitress hospitable. I wanted to sit at a table and ask questions of the conductor, but all six tables were taken, one by the conductor, engineer, and brakeman, but I preferred privacy, and neither the engineer nor the brakeman was a redhead. And they each had two eyes.

"We'll talk on the train," the old conductor said.

Tim and I sat at the counter. We ordered hamburgers, fries, and milkshakes, which we wolfed down as if they were our last meal. The waitress sold us two roundtrip train tickets.

"We usually close at nine, but this being a special occasion, we'll be open all night," she said. "Those who get back after midnight usually drink coffee or nap with their heads on the tables until the morning when the bus pulls in at 7:30."

The train crew got up before I could ask what she meant by *a special occasion*, so Tim and I stood too. We left enough for the bill and a good tip, and followed the men outside to the train. While the engineer and the brakeman climbed up into the cab of the locomotive, we followed the conductor into the caboose.

☾☾☾

"I'm sure you've guessed by now," the conductor said as the train pulled out, "that we come from the same stock."

He removed his cap and ran his fingers through his hair—except on top where he was bald. He looked like a monk, and for a moment I thought it might be a disguise, a skullcap like an actor might wear. He saw our surprise at his baldness.

"My apologies, gentlemen," he said, relaxing in a chair. "I forgot that you've only seen your own and your fathers' hair." He pulled out a pipe and tamped tobacco

into it. "Those of us who live past forty-two tend to go bald around fifty. I'm seventy-three. I'll likely live to be a hundred, possibly a hundred and five. It appears that longevity is the reward for celibacy in our line. A dubious reward, I'd add." He removed his black eye patch and set it on the table.

I stared at the conductor's eyelid, wondering if somewhere he had a green glass eye that his father had passed on to him.

"When we get to Plantation 13," he said, "nobody's going to force you to get off the train. When I was twenty-one, I came here same as you. There were three of us, and I didn't go into town when the other two did. I stayed on the train with the fellow who was the old conductor then. Believe me when I say, *there's no shame in staying on the train.* Even now, I stay aboard when we're in Plantation 13. I've never seen the town, so I can't tell you what's out there. And the boys who make it back don't speak of it. So I don't know, I just don't know. And because I haven't paid my dues, I haven't earned the right to know."

We sat rapt, listening to him.

"But one thing I can say is this: when midnight comes, be on this train, because it pulls out whether you're on it or not. If you're close, I'll pull you aboard if I can. Trust me, you'll want to be on the train. Nobody who's missed it has made the next one two weeks later."

☾☾☾

After an hour's train ride through rugged terrain, the train slowed, and my eyelid began to itch. I was still rubbing it when we pulled to a stop in a broken-down, mist-covered railroad station.

"Plantation 13," the old conductor said from the back porch of the caboose. He made a sweeping arm gesture.

"All ashore that dare go ashore," he said without stepping out onto the station platform himself. "If you'll excuse me, we've got to decouple the log cars on the side track, then do an about-face for the return trip. Stay or go, it's up to you, gentlemen. You've got roughly three hours. Remember what I said. Midnight."

I hesitated a moment, thinking about the bald conductor who expected to live to be a hundred, and about my father—and Tim's father—dying insane at forty-two. Deep inside me, logic battled instinct. I was sure Tim was wrestling with the question, too. After a moment we looked at each other and seemed to draw strength from our new relationship. We climbed down from the train and walked toward the dim streetlights that promised some semblance of a downtown.

Plantation 13's business district was a cross between an Old West ghost town and a 1940s movie set without any automobiles. Main Street was dirt, with a couple of side streets off it. No sidewalks, twenty street lamps total, the downtown's wooden buildings needing either paint, patching, or a wrecking ball. A sign in one window proclaimed a bar inside, another a pool hall. One block contained a hotel, a dry goods store, a hardware store, a drugstore/soda fountain, and a barbershop. As we walked down the center of the street I felt like Burt Lancaster and Kirk Douglas pacing through Tombstone on the way to the gunfight at the OK Corral.

On one corner appeared two women dressed like saloon girls in heavy eye makeup. Three others stepped from the shadows of a side street and slunk toward us, waving, teasing. From the door of the bar came two more, with scarlet feather boas around their shoulders and matching feathered Mae West hats. I could sense others closing the gap behind us, and when we turned, we were surrounded by women. They could have formed a chorus line. They all had flaming red hair like ours, and bewitching green eyes—not one eye but two each. These women were beauties—at least they appeared beautiful to me—captivating, desirable.

"Hey, sweetie," one called kittenishly to Tim, linking her arm with his as if he were her beau. "Movie starts in ten minutes."

She and a half dozen others raised their hands and pointed to the movie house on the next corner. It said MAJESTIC THEATER. Half of the bulbs of its marquee were burned out and nearly all of the letters had fallen off, so that it was impossible to make out what the movie was.

Two women, one on either side of me, clasped my hands in their warm palms and ushered me toward the theater. One looked to be around eighteen, the other fortyish, but both made my pulse race. I could hardly catch my breath.

Tim had his arm around the shoulder of a knockout and was veering toward the theater. We had a huge crowd of women following closely. There was no animosity among them, no possessiveness or fighting over us. It reminded me of World War II, when the men were away and Rosie the Riveter could play. Where were the men who did the logging? But perhaps this was simply ladies' night on the town, my mind said trying to convince myself, and these women were treating us like soldiers and sailors at a USO dance. Whatever was up, the women of Plantation 13 were definitely glad to see us.

The ticket booth at the theater entrance was dark and empty, so we walked right in, all of us, close to a seventy-five by then. The concession stands were dark and cobwebbed, the carpets dusty. But inside, it was just like any old theater. The floor slanted toward a stage, above which hung a huge curtain that would soon uncover a screen when the movie started. The aisles were lit by lamps hidden low on the outside seats, and tarnished brass numbers marked the armrests of the seats.

We poured into the center section of the movie house the way teenagers sometimes do, *en masse*, only with Tim and me—suddenly the most popular kids in school—in the very middle of it all. Dozens of us squeezed into the plush but worn flip-down seats. The only thing missing was popcorn and sodas. And conversation.

I glanced to my right at the younger woman holding my hand, and as I did, I made a mental note of the red EXIT signs that glared at me from either side of the stage.

"Lorraine," the woman purred, as if anticipating my question. "What's yours?" She lightly rubbed my forearm.

I could hardly form words, my mouth was so dry, but finally I croaked out "Arnie."

"Arnie. That's nice," she said, moistening her lips and flaring her nostrils.

The lights dimmed and the curtain opened. In the row ahead of us I heard Tim say, "I'm Tim" to one of the women beside him, and a woman's voice answered, "Tim. That's nice." She lay her head on his shoulder.

A projector lamp flickered behind me somewhere as the curtain in front of us parted, and as it did, a hand caressed the back of my neck. I felt a mix of alarm and pleasure. A moment later the MGM lion roared and the screen came to life as the opening credits rolled. I felt many hands on my arms and shoulders, stroking, massaging, touching lightly. Fingers teased my hair. As my heart raced and the blood pounded in my ears, Lorraine turned to me with longing in her eyes. She opened her lips slightly and her face drew close to mine. I gasped, breathless, then leaned in and met her kiss. It was the most exciting moment of my life.

I couldn't see Tim, but I had no doubt that he, too, was in the throes of a passionate kiss.

Lorraine's tongue probed my lips, and I opened

them slightly for her. My entire body was burning up. She slipped her hands behind my neck and drew me to her, and I wrapped my arms around her and held her close. My eyelid felt warm and pulsed in time with my heartbeat. Lorraine's wet tongue teased mine. I couldn't get enough of it. In that dark theater in Plantation 13 that night, I found myself in another world.

Then suddenly—this is the only way to describe it—*more of her tongue slithered past my lips*, and more of it, and more. It filled my mouth completely, the tip of her tongue gripping my own tongue at its base as if with pliers—*holding me prisoner*—so that I had to inhale and exhale rapid, shallow breaths through my nose. I opened my eye and, even in the dark, could see her green eyes had gone pink, bright pink. They were wide open, glowing, concentrating.

One part of my brain told me I had to remove my arms from her, but another part, something deep down, something instinctive, told me to hold on, and I did. As she filled my mouth with her tongue, I held on for dear life. The movie went on in the background, but it was like being trapped in a dream unable to wake up. It was like hearing and seeing underwater. I had no idea what the movie was about, and I didn't care. I was in a state of euphoria, alternately terrified and thrilled, and I lost any concept of time. In that moment I didn't care about the rest of the world.

As the words THE END came on screen, Lorraine broke free as quickly as she had come on to me, her arms cool and clammy now, her tongue recoiling rapidly the way a vacuum cleaner cord rewinds. My mouth sucked down air in big gulps like a newborn babe spanked to life in a strange new atmosphere.

The entire room breathed then, I could hear it. A collective sigh of relief. Or exhaustion. As the lights came up

slowly, I could see everyone relax, as if they were about to fall asleep after laboring all day in the hot sun.

My eyelid itched and the left side of my head felt heavy, weighted, off-balance. When I put my left hand up to feel my cheek, the cheek was swollen. So was the eyelid. It was puffed out so far that my right eye could see its paunchiness over the bridge of my nose. I felt a migraine building in my head.

From the next row, Tim turned and looked up at me. His eyelid was huge, too, as if a bee sting had caused a severe allergic reaction. We looked hideous.

Suddenly the clapping began. The horde of women started slowly, politely, then gathered intensity and concentration. A rhythm developed, and as they clapped their hands together faster and faster and faster, it was like the beating of bees' wings. The sound was hypnotic, and though something told me to rise and run, something else—a voice from eons past—told me all was as it should be.

Lorraine and the woman with Tim clapped, too, then joined their voices in a high-pitched chant, hands moving with blurring speed now. The others blended in, mouths open, their throats producing a *hreee* sound over and over, like nineteen-year locusts on a summer night.

I felt my eyelid stretching and straining, the flap of skin struggling to contain the swelling behind it. My head and eyelid were about to explode. Suddenly a bolt of pain shot through my cheek and struck a hot nerve deep down behind my empty eye. Then another pain, and another. I couldn't stand it. I yelped and screamed. So did Tim. I stood up. Tim stood up. We wailed together in our agony.

The women ceased their clapping and chanting. The houselights brightened. The entire left side of my face went into a cramp and spasmed.

Suddenly my eyelid burst. So did Tim's. They exploded like piñatas, spewing forth something like wet rice kernels—*maggots*—that hit the warm air of the theater and metamorphosed into dozens and dozens of tiny bat-like creatures. They grasped the gift of flight instantly, instinctively, and swarmed around Tim and me. The warm air agreed with them, and they grew bigger as they swarmed, so that in no time they were each the size of a thumb. And as they expanded, I could see they had faces—*human faces*—with tiny wisps of red hair, and legs and arms that began to sprout from their bodies.

Most had two green eyes, but a dozen or more had only one—*a right eye, the left one hooded,* like mine and Tim's. I wasn't afraid of the newly birthed creatures. In fact, I stood in awe. I felt an attraction, an affinity. Love.

One landed on my shoulder, a one-eyed creature whose arms and legs had just emerged, and it stared up at me like a pup in a shelter, terrified, eyes begging.

The women of Plantation 13 went berserk, scratching and clawing and biting one another to get at the new births, not at the ones on the floor and on the seats that were molting their wings as their lungs filled with oxygen, their bodies swelling and shaping into plump-cheeked, red-haired, green-eyed baby females—*but to get at the one-eyed males,* grabbing the poor things like chicken legs, ripping them apart with their teeth and swallowing them in quick bites.

Suddenly I knew why I was there.

I curled my hand around the pitiful creature on my shoulder, pressed it inside my shirtfront, and began pushing and punching my way through the crimson-mouthed women in their feeding frenzy.

A steam whistle sounded, barely audible over the din in the theater.

"Tim!" I shouted. "The train!"

He shoved two struggling males inside his shirt, and

with elbows and fists fought his way through the hysterical mob. As we started uphill for the lobby, four or five women scuttered over the seats and beat us to the rear door, blocking our retreat.

"There are exits by the stage!" I shouted, and we straight-armed our way through the crowd to the red lights.

Tim flung open the door, and a rush of cold night air whooshed in.

"Down there!" a woman a few paces behind us screamed. "They're stealing them."

We stepped out into the chilly night and Tim slammed the door and held it with his shoulder. The steam whistle sounded again, twice this time. I glanced at my watch. Three minutes.

We ran down the alley, and I heard the door crash open behind us. I knew the women were pouring out of the building behind us, and we had less than twenty yards on them. As we rounded the corner of the Pool Hall building, we glimpsed another horde of flesh-starved women spilling out of the Majestic past the ticket booth.

The steam whistle blasted impatiently. Thank God neither group of women had been able to cut us off from the train. We could see the station, and it all came down to a footrace now. All we had to do was outrun them.

"Here they come! Get them!" someone screamed, and four women stepped out from behind the station platform to block our escape.

"Go through them!" Tim shouted, and we tried to knock them down like they were bowling pins.

Tim went down clutching the precious cargo in his shirt. I had two hands free and punched wildly.

"Get up and fight, Tim!" I cried. "Use your hands."

But they piled on him too fast, and the other two groups of women were almost on us.

"Come on! Run!" I heard the conductor shout. "You're the only one with a chance now. Run!"

The whistle blasted six or eight times in rapid succession then, and I could see the train moving slowly away. It was no longer struggling to overcome its own inertia, now it was rolling steadily forward, picking up speed. I put a hand to my shirt, made sure that my own cargo was still there, and lit out for the tracks. The train looked like it was moving away faster than I was running.

"Run!" the conductor yelled again. "Run!"

I heard the women's voices behind me, but I didn't dare turn to look. Puffing and panting, I managed to match my pace with the train's forward movement, then reached out for the old man's open hand. For a moment I was sure the train had gotten just beyond my reach, but then the old conductor grabbed the handrail, swung himself as far back as he could and clamped his hand around my wrist. I gripped his wrist, too, and he swung me to safety. I looked back and saw my pursuers abandon their footrace.

The conductor ripped up a white sheet for me to use as swaddling cloths and, clearly envious, spent as much time as he could rocking my son. Or perhaps it had been Tim's. I don't know why, but we didn't speak of Tim on the trip back to Eagle Lake. The child cried and slept like any other baby, and by the time we reached the Eagle Lake station, he had plumped up enough that he was pink and fleshy and—except for his webbed left eyelid—looked just like a newborn.

The kindly conductor swabbed the sticky afterbirth fluid from my eye socket and covered it with gauze. He cautioned me not to insert my father's glass eye for at least two full weeks.

"Twenty-one years is what you've got, Arnie," the conductor said the next morning as I boarded the bus

back to Bangor, "if you don't count the year or two of insanity at the end. I wish you and your boy the best."

We waved goodbye, and I wondered if the balding conductor—nearly four times my age, like a doting grandfather who doesn't get to see his grandchildren often enough—was happy with his own life choice. Was there a chance he'd still be the conductor in twenty-one years, when it was my time to become ashes and my son's time to take the night train to Plantation 13?

My eye socket itched under the gauze bandages. But this time it was a different kind of itch. Now it ached for the symbol of fatherhood that had been my father's and my grandfather's and my great-grandfather's, the glass eye. As soon as the socket was healed and ready for it, I'd put it in. And when my time came, as it no doubt would, I would pass it on to the beautiful son who now lay so contently in my arms.

I nearly named the boy Robert. But then I wondered who I'd been named after and why. I named him Tim.

The Tattooist

EVEN THOUGH CHUCK, RAMON, AND I are adults now—big strapping men all over six-feet-four—none of us will go into corner grocery stores or convenience stores late at night, only into large supermarkets with bright lights and plenty of people. And we won't enter a tattoo parlor for love or money.

It was 1963 and we had run away from home, hitch-hiked our way through a series of rides from Eastern Long Island to Elizabeth, New Jersey. I was thirteen, my cousin Chuck and our sidekick Ramon were twelve, and it started because we broke into an old house in our hometown and discovered a wine cellar. We popped the corks on a few dusty bottles and, even though we wouldn't have known if a bottle had gone bad, we did some tasting. The port and chablis and chardonnay, however, didn't satisfy us the way Snickers bars always did. But it seemed silly to let that wine sit there in a deserted house that was about to be torn down. So we absconded with three mixed cases that we hid in our Uncle Edgar's barn two miles away, in a secret attic above the calf pens.

Two days later, on a Saturday morning when we went to check on our stash, we rounded the corner by the calf pens and saw Uncle Edgar's legs on a stepladder, his torso and head up in the secret attic. He'd found us out! And we knew he'd squeal to our parents. We backed out of the calf pen area, ran out of the barn, and lit out for the woods.

It was mid-February, very cold, and several inches of crusted snow covered the ground. Right then and there, at ten o'clock in the morning, we decided the only way out was to run away from home. We convinced ourselves Florida was the place to go. It was warm, we could grab jobs as orange pickers, and we could live on the beach in the warm open air, even at night, until we could find a place to rent. So, without packing so much as a pair of clean underwear, with $6.84 amongst us, we three set out to escape our parents' wrath by thumbing our way to Florida.

Nine hours later, after shivering beside many roads with our thumbs out, and after a hair-raising, high-speed ride down Sunrise Highway with three intoxicated men, we caught our fifth ride, this time with a fiftyish man with a ponytail in an old Volvo. He took us through New York City to Elizabeth, New Jersey—one hundred twenty miles from our starting point.

He was the first one to whom we spilled our story. A big mistake. Shortly after we did that, he yawned, stretched, and pulled off on a dirty side street and parked across from a sleazy diner, saying he needed a cup of coffee if he was going to stay awake.

"Be right back," he said. "Stay in the car. It's not a good part of town to be on foot." Then he crossed the street and disappeared into the diner.

"He's going to call the cops, isn't he?" Chuck said.

"Bet your butt he is," I said.

"We never should have told him," Ramon said. "Now what do we do?" It was seven o'clock, dark, and colder than the afternoon had been.

"Well, either we sit here and wait for the cops to surround the car—which, by the way, means eventually having our parents beat the crap out of us, or," Chuck said, "we make a break for it right now." He put a hand on the door handle, awaiting Ramon's and my decision.

"What the heck," Ramon said. "We've been in a warm car long enough. Florida or bust."

With that, Chuck opened the passenger door and the three of us slipped out, one after the other, and hid behind the car. We checked the diner window to make sure the coast was clear, then fled down the sidewalk and around a corner, running three more blocks before slowing. We walked another ten or fifteen blocks with our collars up and our hands jammed into our pockets.

"Man, it's cold," Chuck said. "We gotta get inside. Maybe there's a Laundromat still open."

"I'm not sure anyone washes their clothes around here," Ramon said.

Many of the buildings were boarded up, while others had broken windows. Only a few had lights. It was how parts of London must have looked during the Blitz.

"We're not in Kansas any more," I said, trying to lighten the mood.

Ramon looked at me stupidly.

"You know," I said. "*The Wizard of Oz?* Dorothy? She says it to her dog, Toto, after they land in Oz. The flying house? The ruby slippers?"

"Oh," Ramon said, rolling his eyes. "Another literary reference, eh? I get it." But he wasn't smiling. None of us was smiling. We were cold and tired and really, really hungry.

"It's time to spend some of our cash," Chuck said. "We've got to eat something. And that'll get us indoors for a while, too. We can warm up. You know, take our time looking for a package of Twinkies." Nobody argued.

On the next corner, just below a burned-out streetlight, we could see what looked like a local neighborhood grocery store. A sign for *Coca Cola* and another proclaiming *Boar's Head Meats* hung in the front window.

A strange, hand-printed sign in the lower corner said: *Tattoos by Bando.*

"Looks like as good a place as any to get Twinkies," Ramon said, so we stepped inside.

"Ah, that heat feels great," Chuck said, and for a moment we just stood soaking it up inside the door. All around us the shelves and the coolers were stocked with the basics—bread, milk, eggs, butter, cream, soda, macaroni, spaghetti, cakes and cupcakes, candy, popcorn and potato chips. I saw a deli case near the back wall, and at one end of it was a counter with a cash register. Behind the counter was an open door that appeared to lead into a back room.

"I don't see anybody," Ramon said. "We could just scoop up a bunch of stuff and run."

That's when a deep ugly voice from the room behind the register said, "Go lock that door before somebody comes in, moron. I told you to do it before."

"Somebody is working," Chuck said.

But something felt wrong. I wanted to grab the door handle and flee, but before I could, a man appeared in the doorway by the counter. He was short and dark-skinned, Cuban or Mexican, possibly an Indian from Central America. His mouth dropped when he saw us, as if we had caught him doing something naughty. The look quickly became a forced smile.

"Well, hello, boys. Didn't hear you there. Come in, come in. We're still open." As he spoke, he edged around the corner of the counter and strode down the aisle. "What can I help you with?"

"Uh, nothing," I said, but Ramon cut me off.

"Twinkies," he said.

"Sure," the man said. "No problem." He reached for the door with his left hand, not letting us see his right hand and arm. "Shop around. I've just got to lock up. Closing time, you know? You'll be my last customers."

"Great," Ramon said. "That'll give us a minute to

warm up, too. It's getting really cold out there." Ramon didn't seem to sense that something was amiss.

"Okay, but not too long," the man said, not leaving the door. He yelled toward the back room, "It's okay, Dad, just three boys come in to get some Twinkies." Then he nodded, trying to appear pleasant. "Go ahead, one pack of Twinkies each. There's no charge tonight. I've already emptied the cash register." Something told me he had, too.

"Wow! Free Twinkies," Ramon said, his eyebrows arching in surprise and delight. "Somebody's watching over us tonight." I sure hoped so.

Another man, nearly six feet tall, with a black mustache and an acne-scarred face, appeared in the back doorway. He was too close in age to the first man to be the father. And his coloring was different, he was paler, so he couldn't be a brother. Something wasn't right.

"We hate to hurry you, boys," the man with the mustache said without smiling, "but we have to close." His face looked tense, his words rang hollow.

Ramon grabbed three packs of Twinkies from a shelf and walked toward the register. What was he thinking? The first man had said we could take them for free.

"The man by the front door told us we could have the Twinkies free," Ramon said. "Could we also get some water?"

The man's eyes narrowed as he glared at his companion by the front door.

Suddenly a moan arose from the back room, then "Police. Call the police."

Ramon's eyes flicked toward the back room, then back to the scar-faced man. I sneaked a sideways glance at Chuck. His eyes had grown wide, his mouth making an O. The two of us turned for the front door and saw the short man's fingers on the latch.

Click! He had locked us in.

"Sorry, boys," he said. "I tried to give you an out. But it's a case of wrong time, wrong place."

A wicked grin came over his face then and I felt a chill run down my spine. He raised his right hand from behind his body and light glinted off something. Polished steel! A machete!

"Back room, boys!" he ordered. "Pronto."

The back room was square, about twenty by twenty, with no back door or window, only a heavy door with a huge handle on it built into the wall. I was pretty sure it

was a walk-in cooler like Uncle Edgar had in the milk house at the farm. No escape except the way we'd come in. A small plank table sat in the middle of the room with a single three-bulb light fixture above it. It looked like it was set up for a card game, except there were only three chairs. An old man lay slumped in a corner to our right. Blood trickled from the corner of his mouth and from his forehead.

"Get 'em into the cooler, Chico," the man with the mustache said, nodding toward the heavy door. "No sound in there."

The short, dark man raised his machete menacingly and we moved toward the door, Chuck in the lead.

"Can't," Chuck said, placing a hand on the heavy door handle. "It's locked." A heavy-duty padlock secured it.

"Watch 'em," the man with the mustache said, then reached down and grabbed the old man by the front of his shirt. He lifted him to his feet and slammed him against the wall. "All right, old man, where's the key?" he snarled.

The old man's head hung down, his chin on his chest. His tormentor shook him and then slapped his face.

"Wake up, old man," he hissed. "Where's the key to the cooler?"

The old man raised his head a little, shook out the cobwebs. "I don't have it. The owner locks it at night before he goes home."

"The owner? Then who are you?" the man snarled, lifting the old man off the ground even higher by his shirtfront.

The old man wore his gray-black hair in a ponytail, and in the dim light I thought he looked Middle Eastern, possibly even Italian or Greek. But then again, he could have been from the Philippines. It was hard to pin down. He was like the actor, Anthony Quinn, who played a

Mexican, an Indian, a Greek, an Italian, and many other parts.

"I'm Bando, the tattooist. The neighborhood kids call me Uncle Bando. The grocer lets me use this room to practice my art when someone comes seeking a fine tattoo. Instead of rent, I tend the store the last hour of each night so the owner can spend time with his family. You gentlemen chanced to come in the last hour before closing. I don't have the key to the cooler, it's on the grocer's key ring."

Apparently satisfied, the bully relaxed his grip and let Bando stand on his own.

"What now?" the man with the machete said. "They've seen our faces."

The scar-faced man didn't seem to know what to do.

"You have the money from the cash register," Bando said. "You can also take whatever groceries you can carry. So you've got what you came for, right? There's nothing else here of interest to the two of you, is there? *Unless, of course, you've come for a tattoo.*"

Wham! The short man buried his machete blade in the tabletop the way an ax bites into a stump. "Idiot!" he spat. "You stupid old man, do we look like we came in for a tattoo?"

I could see the old man's eyes from across the room. No fear, no emotion. Crazy as it may sound, his face appeared *relaxed,* as if he'd expected this. And for a moment, just for a moment, his eyes seemed to show pity for the man grasping the machete handle.

"Truthfully? Yes," Bando said in a calm, measured voice. "You do look like you came in for a tattoo. And if you release these boys, the tattoo is on the house."

The short man glared at him, then looked up at the other man. "Is he stupid, or what?"

The man with the mustache shrugged and half smiled at Bando's audacity. "He's got guts, I'll say that for him."

"Sit down, gentlemen," the tattooist said, motioning them to the plank table. "You on this side, you on the other side. I have a very unusual pattern to show you, *shared artwork*, one especially designed for brothers-in-arms."

The machete blade remained buried in the tabletop.

"There are hundreds of examples of my work pictured here," Bando continued, gesturing toward a thick loose-leaf binder on the table. "But I think you'll want to check the last page." He flipped the binder open. "This one."

The two hoods gasped.

"That's incredible," the short one said.

"Awesome," the other added.

Chuck, Ramon, and I leaned in for a closer look. A full-page color photograph showed an incredibly detailed tattoo of a skull with two snakes entwined around each other, their slithering bodies twisted through the eye sockets, nose and mouth holes, and ears. But upon closer examination I could see that the grinning death's head was actually two tattoos, a pair of practically seamless images making up a whole. The men in the picture were using their right hands to clasp each other's biceps above the elbow, so that their right forearms were side-by-side except facing in opposite directions. When fitted together, the individually tattooed forearms made up a single larger image. It was like a pirate movie in which the two ripped halves of a treasure map were pieced together to reveal the secret hiding place. In the tattoo, the snakes' brilliant swirling colors reminded me of gas and oil slicks on the water by the docks, and the grinning skull looked like it might speak at any moment.

"That is my famous *Brothers-in-Arms Tattoo*," Bando said. "I've done it only once, and that was in Vietnam for the two mercenaries you see in the photo."

"Incredible," uttered the man with the mustache, mesmerized. He glanced across the table at his partner. "Whaddya think, Chico? Should we go for it?"

"Nobody else in Jersey will have anything like it. I'm game if you are. But what about them?" The short man nodded toward us. "And the old man?" His eyes narrowed as he and his partner each sneaked a sideways look at the machete.

"I said I'd do the tattoo if you let the boys go," Bando said. "You must promise."

The hoods looked at each other coldly.

"Oh, all right, we promise," said the scar-faced one, his voice condescending. "And you, too. But only if you four promise not to turn us in." He smiled, and I noticed that one of his eyeteeth was missing.

Bando quietly said, "Last month a storekeeper was killed on the East Side. He was hacked to death during a robbery gone sour. Nothing to do with you two, right?"

Was this old man crazy? These two had said they'd let us all go if we promised not to turn them in to the cops for the robbery. Now he'd made it clear he knew they were also murderers. How could they let us go after that?

"Couldn't have been us," the short man said. "We both had alibis. I was with him, and he was with me." He grinned broadly.

The scar-faced man nodded. "It's the God's-honest truth. We were together."

Bando's mouth curled into a cryptic smile. "Very well, gentlemen," he said. "Then let's proceed. First we must wash down your arms with alcohol to reduce the risk of infection."

The men rolled up their sleeves.

"Boys," the tattooist said, "grab my leather bag and the bottle of alcohol next to it, right there on the shelf."

Ramon reached for the bottle and I pulled down the

bag. The bag was heavy, as if it contained a couple of sacks of nails.

"Just a minute!" the scar-faced man said. He reached behind him and slammed the door that led out to the store, then placed his right hand on the left side of his belt and pulled out his own machete. "Just in case," he said. "No tricks!" He swung the glinting blade above his head and buried it in the tabletop.

With both men having quick access to machetes, we had little hope of escape. And I knew, once they had their tattoo, they wouldn't keep their promise.

"May I have my bag now?" the old man said. "And the alcohol?"

"Here, Mr. Bando," Ramon said as we placed the alcohol and the bag on the table.

"You boys can call me Uncle Bando. As I said, all the kids around here do."

We nodded and said weakly, "*Uncle* Bando."

Uncle Bando opened the leather bag and withdrew what looked to be a large, heavy bib, the kind they put over your chest when they X-ray you, except this had a square cut out of the center. It reminded me of something surgeons might use in an operating room, so only the opened-up area would be exposed.

"Gentlemen, you'll need to join your forearms as in the photograph—a Roman centurion's salute, a very manly greeting. Grip your friend's lower biceps muscle. Once you lock arms, though, you mustn't move. I'll scrub your arms with alcohol and then we'll lay this leaded mat over your arms. There's less chance you'll tremble that way. Are you ready?"

"Don't you have to shave our arm hairs?" the short man said.

"Not necessary."

The tattooist waited.

The short man gave a what-the-heck shake of his

head and placed his right forearm on the table. The man with the mustache did the same and they looked as if they were about to grip hands and arm wrestle. Instead they locked arms in the Centurion's salute.

"You don't have to squeeze," Uncle Bando said. "If you do, your muscles will tire and your arms will be shaking soon."

He took a cloth from the bag, poured alcohol on it, and swabbed the men's arms. Then he draped the leaded bib over them from elbow to elbow. The bib was the perfect length, as if it had been custom made for the length of the two men's arms. The tattooist used Velcro straps to secure it around each man's elbow. It resembled a sling for a broken arm, except this one was double-ended.

The men leaned toward the center of the table to peer inside the open square, but their heads blocked the overhead light and cast shadows over the opening so they couldn't see anything.

"Sit up straight and relax, gentlemen. There will be a little pain. But you're tough, you two, you're street-hardened, and you can take it. And no need to worry, you can easily reach your machetes."

For a moment I considered snatching up the machetes, but I wasn't sure we had the strength to pull the blades free. And I knew we didn't have what it took to use them on the men.

Uncle Bando withdrew another cloth from his bag, this one brown and only slightly larger than a washcloth. It looked soft, like a chamois cloth for polishing a bowling ball. He placed it over the square opening. Then—and this I didn't anticipate at all—he bowed his head, closed his eyes, and began rubbing his hands together as if washing them. But he had no alcohol on them. I guess he was creating energy.

"Where's the needles, doc?" the short man said with a nervous laugh.

"And the ink?" the scar-faced man said.

"That's not the way I work," Uncle Bando said.

He placed his hands on the soft cloth and began kneading it and the tissue beneath it, like a masseuse, his fingers opening and closing the way a cat flexes its claws.

Both men grimaced. It didn't look like Uncle Bando was massaging their flesh, it appeared he was simply working the soft cloth. Why were they wincing?

"The pain's not too much for you, is it, gentlemen?" he asked, smiling slyly, his eyes still closed as he worked.

"No," the man with the mustache said through gritted teeth.

"How long does this take?" the short man said. "And once it's softened up, when do you start with the needles?"

"About another minute, that's all. And no needles. Just another minute."

Perhaps I imagined it, but I thought I heard the faint sounds of cracking and grinding, like a tree branch rubbing against another limb in the wind.

And then it was over. Uncle Bando pulled his hands away, made them into a steeple in front of his face, thumbs touching his chin, fingers touching his nose as if in prayer, and he stood up from the chair.

"Finished, gentlemen," he said. He plucked the cloth from the square hole, folded it and placed it in his bag. "Ready to see the magic?" He grasped two corners of the leaded bib like a magician about to whisk a handkerchief off a top hat.

The men nodded, their faces relaxed now that the pain was over.

Uncle Bando lifted off the leaded bib.

"What the—?" both men gasped, and Chuck, Ramon, and I gasped, too.

There before us was the Brothers-in-Arms Tattoo.

But it was different from the one in the photograph.

The one in the looseleaf binder had shown *two arms.* What lay before us on the table—shared by the men—was a *single tattooed forearm.* The hands and wrists had disappeared, and from one man's elbow to the other's elbow was nothing but a solitary arm covered by the skull-and-snakes tattoo.

"Time for us to go, boys," Uncle Bando said, calmly buckling the clasp on his bag as he motioned us toward the door.

We opened the door and stepped out into the store, leaving the stunned hoods staring down at their arm. Uncle Bando hustled us toward the front door.

"Boys," he called, walking toward us with the three packs of Twinkies. "Don't forget these. Eat them on the way to the precinct house, four blocks that way. Call your parents from there. They'll be relieved."

Later, on the ride home, we would recall that Uncle Bando didn't know we were runaways.

"What should we tell the cops about those guys in the store? What should we say happened?" Chuck said.

"I wouldn't even mention them," Uncle Bando said. "They've got their machetes with them and they have a very tough choice to make. Sad to say, but they have a history of making poor choices."

Uncle Bando stepped back inside the store for a moment, reached into the front window, grabbed his handmade *Tattoos by Bando* sign, and closed the door again as he left. We waved goodbye to him and started through the frigid night for the police station.

Uncle Bando was right about the men making bad decisions. Before we got a block from the store, we heard two horrible screams pierce the air. We took off running.

The Chair

MY TWIN SISTER STEPHANIE and I found the old chair at The Junque Shoppe, a place that was a cross between a Salvation Army thrift store and a pawnshop. We bought it for eight dollars. I coughed up five bucks and my sister kicked in three. We needed the chair for our tree house, which didn't have much for furnishings. This gray metal armchair was perfect and would complement the small wooden chair our mother had given us.

So that day, a bright sunny day without a cloud in the sky, we walked down the street in Norwich like we were on top of the world, lugging our new purchase. First Steph would carry it half a block, then I'd carry it half a block. It was heavy as all get-out, but we were sure it would be worth the effort.

I was carrying it past the library when I felt a tingling in my wrists. Because it was so heavy and awkward, I had it propped up on my back, my wrists resting on my shoulders as I gripped it by its seat back. I wasn't quite sure what the feeling was—like a pinched nerve maybe (but one in each wrist?)—and I had to set it down. It felt like I'd hit the funny bone in my elbow, except that this wasn't just the elbows but was in my wrists and hands and fingertips, too. It was like when your leg goes to sleep and you try to walk on it.

"What's the matter?" Steph said.

"Strange feeling in my arms." I rested an arm on the seatback as I stood there. I flexed the other, hoping it'd help get the circulation back, which it did. Right away

that arm stopped tingling. But the one still resting on it didn't.

"We can wait," Steph said, sitting down in the chair.

No sooner had she sat on it than something shot through the tingly arm that was still in contact with the chair. It was a mix of *physical* pain and *emotional* pain. It was so strange to feel, and even stranger to realize the pains were so different. But it was like hitting your thumb with a hammer—that's physical pain—and feeling sad about your dog being hit by a car—that's emotional.

What else was weird was, this was *my* pain, but at the same time it *wasn't* mine. When my sister sat in that chair, my cheeks and face felt sore and swollen, the way they had when I sledded into a tree trunk and had to go to the hospital. But I also felt fearful, terrified, and found it difficult to breathe. Again it was *my* fear and *my* labored breathing, yet it *wasn't* mine.

I had a sudden image of a woman whose face I couldn't make out, her wrists and ankles bound to the chair with electrical cord. Her head was lolled toward me onto her left shoulder, and I could see a trickle of blood coming from her nose. I saw what appeared to be a mouth gag—actually, it was silver duct tape—but I knew the woman was still breathing, though shallowly through her nose. On a wall in the distance a large clock read 12:10.

"Get up," I gasped, not sure myself who I was speaking to. "Get up."

Steph turned and looked up at me. She raised herself from the chair, but she kept hold of its arm.

"Let go!" I said.

She did, and the vision in my head vanished.

I pulled my right hand off the chair then, and the tingling disappeared as quickly as the image of the woman had. My hands were trembling.

THE CHAIR

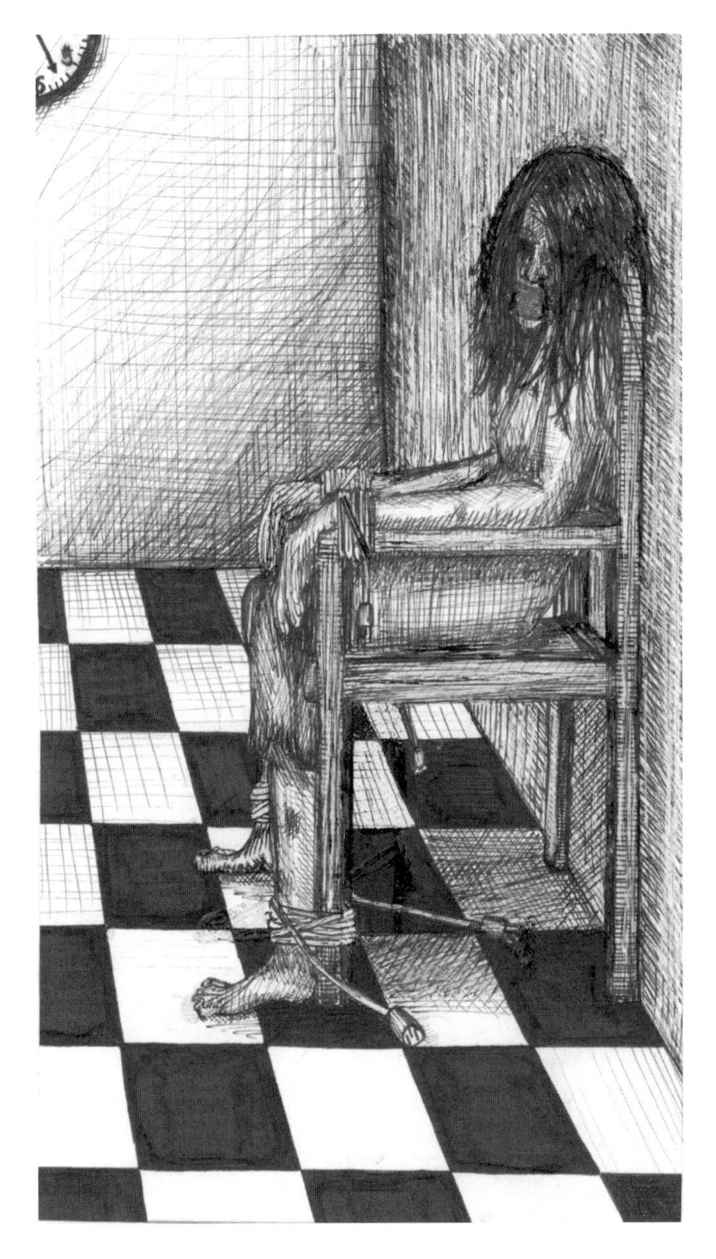

"You okay?" Steph said, staring.

"Don't touch it," I warned. "There's something weird about it."

"The chair's weird?" she said. "I think you're the one who's weird."

I told her about the vision of the woman. "I'm pretty sure she was unconscious. And she had two black eyes, like from being punched. I think her nose was broken, too. It was horrible. It was so real."

"I'll carry it awhile," she said, reaching for the chair.

"No!" I swatted her hand, and when she reached again, I grabbed her wrist. "Don't touch it! I don't know what it is, but it's coming from that chair."

"Baloney!" she said, and flicked my hand away. She picked it up and slung it over her shoulder so the legs were pointing straight up in the air. "I'll be the mule for awhile. Let's go."

By the time she was ten feet ahead of me on the sidewalk, both arms had fully returned to normal and I felt the color coming back into my face.

"Anything happening?" I asked when I caught up.

"Nope. Feels like a chair. Getting heavy. You carry it the next block."

"I don't think I can," I said. "Seriously."

Despite the fact that we were twins, my sister wasn't always sensitive to me. But this time, for some reason, she sensed my deep reluctance and didn't insist I carry it. With occasional stops, she lugged the chair all the way to the tree house.

The tree house was in a small wooded area near our neighborhood on the south end of Norwich. There were no homes near the woods, which was why we chose the spot. I climbed the ladder to the trap door, opened it and climbed up, then lowered a piece of clothesline to tie onto our prize.

"Ready?" she called up. "I push, you pull."

While I pulled the rope, she grabbed the chair's legs to keep it from spinning. When it was within reach, I grasped it by the top of its seatback—the same place I had touched it before. No strange feeling this time, not yet anyway. Steph supported its weight from the bottom and I wrestled it up through the trap door and inside. But before I could let go, the tingling started, and I couldn't let myself release it. Maybe I didn't want to.

The tiny electrical charges crept into my fingers and a picture flashed in my mind—a heavyset man with black hair and mustache who looked like the migrant workers I'd seen working the farms in the summer. He was lying on a cot with a clock on the wall above him. I knew it was the same clock. This vision faded and I was finally able to let go of the seatback.

"You okay?" Steph said, climbing up through the trapdoor. "You're white as a ghost."

I told her what I'd seen.

"Let me try it," she said, and I showed her where to place her hands.

"Anything?" I said.

"No tingling. No visions." She closed her eyes.

"Here," I said. "Let me help you." I placed my hands on hers. Immediately I felt the tingling start, first in my fingers and palms, then up my forearms, like heat this time.

"I feel it," she said. "It's like static electricity passing from the chair through my hands to yours."

"See anything?" I said. "I don't this time. Maybe it's stopping with you."

"No. I can't see anything, but I can hear. I hear a woman's voice, very faint. Sounds like she's hurt. No clear words, though. It's like I'm underwater, like how sounds were muted when we knocked rocks together on the bottom during swimming lessons. Remember? But I'll bet this is the same woman you saw."

I couldn't hear a thing. Somehow my sister, even though she couldn't pick up any vibes directly from the chair the way I could, was able to hear through my contact. Once I touched the chair and she touched me, she could hear what I could see.

"Maybe it's like putting D-batteries in a radio," she said. "Four face one direction, four face the other direction."

"And the positive and negative need to line up," I reminded.

We experimented with several new combinations in addition to mine on hers. We tried her hands on mine, then our hands next to each other so that all four were in direct contact with the seatback. Then a stack of four—hers, mine, hers, mine—and vice versa. Eventually we tried my right hand on the seatback with hers on top and her left hand on the seatback with mine on top, an alternating pattern that, like a radio turned the right way, seemed to draw the strongest signal.

With that combination, we felt energy in no time and connected to something or someone somewhere. I saw the clock on the wall again, watched it silently jump from 12:45 to 12:46.

Steph heard it. *Tick*.

I was seeing snatches of this scene from who-knew-where, and she was hearing them.

The man lying on the cot reached for a whiskey bottle beside him on the floor. The worn tiles made up a checkerboard pattern of dirty black and white. The cot was a fold-up metal one, the mattress thin. No sheets, no pillow, only a gray army blanket. The man's uniform was gray and reminded me of the overalls the grease monkeys wore at the station Dad took the car to for oil changes. Three chairs identical to ours sat against the wall near the cot.

I moved my hands and tried shifting the position of

my head and body in hopes of getting a better view of the room. But it was like watching somebody else's videotape. I wasn't in control of the camera; my face was stuck in one spot—like looking out a windowpane—and my viewpoint was limited.

"She moaned again," Steph said. "Can you see her?"

The camera in my mind panned from the cot to the woman in the chair. I could see the top of her head, then the left side, as she tried to raise it from her left shoulder.

"She's coming to," I said.

"A man coughed," Steph said, and the focus swung back to the man on the cot.

He sat up, lit a cigarette. Steph was right. He was coughing. I could see it but there was no sound. It was like I was deaf inside the scene, though I could hear Steph in our world. The man pulled a cigarette pack from his shirt pocket and tried to shake out a smoke, then crumpled the empty pack and threw it aside in disgust.

"He crushed something made of paper, didn't he?" Steph said.

"Yeah. A cigarette pack. He threw it on the floor. It landed next to a butcher knife there."

"Do you think this has already happened?" Steph said. "Are we tapping into the chair's history? Or is this actually happening someplace?"

"I don't know," I said, pulling my hands away. "But we can't just keep watching. We've got to get help."

☾☾☾

"You have to hurry," Steph told the cop at the desk after we'd told him our story. "This woman is in danger."

"He may be killing her right now," I said, and felt guilty even saying the words, as if uttering them out loud might make them come true.

The cop was an older man with gray hair and reminded me of our grandfather. He didn't laugh at what we we'd said, in fact he seemed to take us seriously. We had expected our story to be discounted by grownups, especially the skeptical police—two kids cooking up a whopper to get attention. We'd seen Disney movies. But he said the Norwich Police Department had on several occasions consulted a famous local psychic—with mixed results—so the police force was somewhat familiar with parapsychology and the paranormal.

"But assuming this is a crime in progress or one that's already happened, we still have no way of knowing who we're looking for or where to look," he said. "Am I right?"

Steph looked at me blankly.

"The chair," I said. "The chair in the tree house is the connection."

"So what is it you want me to do, send a patrolman out to watch you read the chair?"

A woman in a police uniform appeared at the door.

"I couldn't help overhearing, Sarge. Hello, kids. This is fascinating stuff. Getting vibrations or energies from an object is called *telekinesis*. It's what our consulting psychic did on that missing child case last year."

"Yeah," the sergeant said. "She held this kid's teddy bear and in her mind saw him wandering around up on Reservoir Road in Taftville. It was like a bloodhound getting a scent, or like following a DNA trail. Can't explain it, but it was amazing to see."

"What's unusual with these two," the woman cop said, "is that it involves not just *telekinesis* with the chair, but two other phenomena. This young man says he's getting messages transmitted by some entity in another realm—and by another realm I mean someplace else *spatially, geographically,* or possibly even somewhere else *in time*. What he seems to be experiencing is called *clairvoyance* or *clear seeing*. His sister

seems to be manifesting *clairaudience* or *clear hearing*. And maybe because they're twins—we know twins have special connections—they're attuned to the same scene. I can't say for sure."

"This is why she's the Chief of Police and I'm the sergeant," the older cop said, playing dumb. "College. Book learning."

The woman smiled and said to the sergeant. "We don't know if there's anything to this, but I doubt these two could make this up. First, they'd have nothing to gain. Second, it's a complicated story, and it's just crazy enough to be something. Let's have one of our guys check out the chair in the tree house. And get somebody else over to The Junque Shoppe. Find out what the owner knows about the chair, and where he got it."

"Right away, Chief," the sergeant said, and the woman left the room. He walked around the desk. "Come on. I'll introduce you to Officer Riggins. You can have your first ride in a police car."

☾☾☾

Five minutes later we were back in our tree house.

"You want me to examine the chair up there?" Officer Riggins, the baby-faced cop, said. "Or do you want to lower it down? I can climb up, no problem."

"Maybe we should take it to the station." Steph said.

"Nah," Riggins said. "I just need to see if there's any identifying data on it."

"But maybe there are bloodstains that are barely visible," I said. "Maybe someone was murdered in it. Shouldn't it go to a crime lab?"

"I can tell you two watch a lot of TV," he said. "If we turn up a crime, we can always come back for it. Bloodstains won't go anywhere. For the time being we're simply looking to see where it can lead us."

"Okay," Steph said. "We'll tie the rope on and lower it down."

As I was tying the line around it, Steph called down to Officer Riggins, "We'd better check in first."

"With your parents?" he said.

"No. With the woman," I answered knowing that's what Steph was going to say.

We placed our hands on the seatback as we had before, and the tingling crept in immediately.

"She's crying," Steph said.

The baby-faced cop quietly observed us.

The man with the mustache was standing before the woman tied in the chair. She didn't have the duct tape over her mouth this time. He slapped her face.

"Somebody spit at somebody," Steph said.

"Yeah. She spit in his face. I saw it."

"Now he's slapped her again. I heard the first one, and now another. It was almost a punch this time."

"Yeah," I said.

We let go of the chair and lowered it to Riggins, then climbed down while he examined it.

"Gun metal gray, like something you'd find on a military base, like the Sub Base in Groton," he said, "or in a government office. It's too uncomfortable to be from a hospital or doctor's office. No serial numbers, just a black stencil: NSH. Could be someone's name, a company name, or a place. If it was government, it'd say US GOVT or USN for Navy."

"She's still alive," Steph said. "I can feel it."

As we walked back toward the patrol car, Officer Riggins stopped, turned back and grabbed the chair. "Whatever you two have is catching. Something tells me we need to bring this back to the station."

Steph smiled at him, and he shrugged. "Hey, I can always drive it back if we don't need it, right?"

☾☾☾

"Sarge," said a cop who walked into the station. "I met with the junk shop owner. He buys a chair every couple of months. He pays three dollars a chair, resells them for five to ten. The guy's been bringing them in one at a time for years. Shop owner says he's gone through two or three dozen, identical. He doesn't know where they come from, but he doesn't think they're hot."

"They come from NSH," Officer Riggins said, tipping the chair to show the others the stencil. "Wherever that is. What do you think—National Security Something?"

The three cops tossed out a few possibilities, and the sergeant jotted a list on a notepad.

"If it started with the word National," the Chief cut in, it'd be familiar to one of us. "The N isn't National."

Riggins nudged Steph and me toward the chair. We put our hands on it. I closed my eyes, hoping that better concentration might hurry an image along.

"She's trying to scream," Steph said. "But it's muted. I think he's put the duct tape over her mouth again. No one can hear her except that man and me."

"He's waving the butcher knife in front of her, taunting her," I said. "Now he's coming my way, he's taking a drink of whiskey, setting the bottle on a table right in front of my nose. The table, the bottle, it's all only a few inches from my face. He's using the knife to shave the hairs off his forearm, to show her how sharp it is. He's picking up the bottle again, another drink. I can almost touch him he's so close. What do you hear, Steph?"

"I don't hear a thing. Nothing."

"Look around the room," the Chief said. "What else can you see? Walls, doors, anything distinctive?"

"I can only see what's in front of me. I'm seeing through somebody else's eyes, and I can't make my head turn the way I could if I was there in the room. To the far left it reminds me of that TV show about the bar in Boston."

"*Cheers*," the sergeant said.

"Why's it remind you of *Cheers*?" the Chief said.

"It's like that door, the way they came in and went out. I think there's a frosted window to its left. Something tells me there are stairs outside the door, stairs going up, like in *Cheers*. I can't see it, but it's an impression."

"So we're in a basement," the baby-faced cop said. "What else do you see?"

"Across the room, a map. No, a diagram, on the wall: B-7 FIRE ESCAPE ROUTE.

"Basement. Seven," the sergeant said. "Building Seven basement. But where?"

"Maybe the N is for Norwich," Riggins said. "NSH. Norwich SH."

"He just put his cigarette out in water," Steph said. "I heard it hiss."

"And when you said that, Steph," I said, "my vision flinched like somebody yelled boo behind me. Whatever camera I'm seeing this through, whoever's eyes, was startled when that cigarette hissed out."

"Norwich State Hospital!" Riggins said. "The old mental hospital. The State shut it down in 1996. Those buildings have been empty for a decade. That's where he gets the chairs."

"Sarge, keep the kids here," the Chief said. "You two," she said to the officers. "Let's go. Basement, Building Seven. Sarge, get any other cars in that area to the scene. No lights, no sirens."

☾☾☾

The Norwich Police got there just in time. The woman had a broken nose, cheekbone, wrist, and a con-

cussion, but she was alive and would recover. The chair thief had been a janitor at the State Hospital for two years before it closed, but he made copies of his keys. He planned to kill the woman. That same night he was arrested, he confessed to murdering another woman, his ex-girlfriend, in the same basement eight months earlier. Traces of her blood were discovered on our chair.

Steph and I never saw the basement room. We didn't want to. But Officer Riggins and the Chief told us that when they broke into the basement room of Building Seven, they saw the table that had provided my vantage point. The whiskey bottle—the one the man had set down inches from my nose—was still sitting there. Directly behind the bottle—where Officer Riggins said he expected to see a camcorder—sat a fish tank filled with water. Floating on top was the disintegrating cigarette Steph had heard the man snuff out. And swimming back and forth in the fish tank, pausing occasionally to survey the scene, was a tiny pop-eyed goldfish.

The Chambers Crypt

"WELL, WELL. If it isn't Devaney and Hoag, couch potatoes," my wife Carol said as she and her mother came in from church and took their coats off. My father-in-law and I knew better than to engage her. It was close to lunchtime and experience had taught us if we didn't antagonize her, she and her mother would make us all lunch.

"You've got to get out more often boys," my mother-in-law said. "We got out today, maybe that's why we scooped you."

Devaney and I turned away from the television and our wives flashed those smug, cat-that-ate-the-canary smiles.

"What do you mean, *scooped* us?" Devaney said.

"Well," Carol said. "If you'd go to church once in awhile, you might be there when a story breaks."

I'm a reporter for the *Valley News*, the daily that serves both White River Junction, Vermont and Lebanon, New Hampshire, and the small towns clustered around that part of the Connecticut River's Upper Valley. Mostly I write local news, human-interest stories, and features. My father-in-law, Devaney, a retired history teacher, is a pretty decent amateur photographer who keeps me company and shoots most of my pictures.

"Yeah, like a lot of stories break out at church," Devaney guffawed, seemingly unaware he was killing our chances for lunch.

"As a matter of fact, Mr. Smarty," my mother-in-law said, "a story did break in church today."

Devaney smiled a tight smile, rolled his eyes with feigned disinterest.

"What story?" I said.

Carol paused, pretending she might not spill it. But she'd obviously been dying to tell us since she got in the door.

"Ghosts," she said, letting the word hang.

Devaney and I sat up.

"Oh, come on," I said. "You're talking about the Holy Ghost, right? Church talk. On the third day rising from the dead, that kind of ghost."

Carol looked at her mother, then back at us. "No, we're not talking about church stuff, although these are church-related. We're talking about ghosts, real ghosts. In Norwich."

"Norwich?" Devaney barked out. "Where? Who saw them?"

My father-in-law and I had accumulated a number of stories (*cases*, he prefers to call them, but since I write them up for the paper, I call them stories) in and around Norwich, Vermont. Ever since we'd gotten involved with the Norwich Witch and the Witness Tree on the green there, locals had begun treating us not just as reporter and photographer, but as *psychic detectives* (though neither of us is psychic). Some folks even use the terms *ghost busters*, though we've never busted any ghosts. Now, whenever something weird or out of the ordinary happens—a cow or pet disappearance, a freshly cracked or toppled tombstone, an eerie mist over a swampy area—we get phone calls. Not from my editor (except on special occasions), but directly from townspeople, sometimes in the middle of the night.

"Gee, Mom, I don't know about you," Carol said. "But I'm getting hungry. Must be close to lunchtime." I

could see a twinkle in Carol's eye. "Sure would be nice to have somebody else fix Sunday lunch for a change, wouldn't it?" My wife stared right at me and waited, close-mouthed.

"That would be a real treat," her mother said. "Maybe you men would consider preparing lunch and *serving us* on this Sabbath day of rest." She stared at Devaney exactly the way Carol was staring at me.

Twenty minutes later the four of us sat around the kitchen table, a plate of my tuna-with-celery sandwiches in the center along with a saucer of dill pickles. Bowls of tomato soup and glasses of iced tea sat in front of us.

"Okay," I said, plunking a bag of potato chips on the table as I sat down. "Lunch is served. Now it's your turn, ladies. What's this about ghosts?"

"Ahem," my mother-in-law said, folding her hands. "Perhaps we could offer thanks for the meal first. It's been awhile since we've done that, I believe. What do you say, Carol?"

Carol nodded and turned to me. "Honey, would you say grace?"

Devaney exhaled heavily at the blackmail. I simply smiled and we all bowed our heads. I thanked God for the food, the hands that had so lovingly prepared such a masterpiece, and for the loving spouses we all had. Devaney said Amen and we divvied up the sandwiches.

"Well," Carol started. "Everybody at church was talking about what happened up at the Congregational Church in Norwich, the one on the green."

Devaney and I had been there before, for our first "case." When the church bell began humming of its own accord, Town Constable Dutch Roberts and we had met with Reverend Halliday, who let us go up inside the bell tower to investigate.

"It seems there was a Junior Youth Group meeting in the church last night. The children are fifth and sixth graders. The leaders, two couples in their thirties, took the kids for an after-dark hike down the road to the River Bend Cemetery."

Devaney shot me a look that said we'd given in too early on fixing lunch. It was obvious where this story was going—youth group, ancient graveyard, black of night.

"Well, nothing happened at the cemetery. They went for their hike—eight of them and their four advisors—then came back. Around eight o'clock they all went to the minister's house for hot chocolate. The minister wasn't there, he was away for a conference, but his wife was there. She had a roaring fire in the fireplace. While they were sitting around it, one of the girls saw something in the fire—*people*, she said, *four* of them. The other kids swore they saw them, too."

I cast a sideways glance at Devaney. He was looking at me out of the corner of his eye in the same doubting way.

"But here's the kicker," my mother-in-law said. "*The adults saw them, too*."

A chill ran down my spine. The chill never failed to alert me to a real story.

"That's right," Carol said. "The kids, the four advisors, and the minister's wife—thirteen people—all swear four people were calling to them out of the flames."

I looked at Carol and saw she wasn't trying to pull the wool over our eyes. We didn't know what had actually occurred, but she and her mother seemed convinced there was something to the story. And I had my chill—*my hunch*— to rely on.

"And what were they calling out, these four ghosts?" Devaney said.

"I don't know," Carol said, glancing around at her mother, who shrugged her shoulders, too. "I guess nobody got that part of the story. You think it's important?"

"Important? I'm not even convinced anything *really* happened," I said, only half-lying. "At least, anything to do with ghosts. But it seems to me, if they were calling out something, they might like us to listen to whatever it is they're trying to tell us, don't you think?"

Carol and her mother agreed, and we rehashed the details several times over lunch. Then Devaney and I called the minister's wife in Norwich and arranged an interview for three o'clock. She gave us the names and numbers of the two couples who were the advisors, and we set up meetings with them for four and five o'clock. If the story seemed like it was worth pursuing further, we'd get information on the eight kids and interview them separately over the next couple of days.

☾☾☾

"Of course we were frightened, all of us," Mrs. Halliday, the pastor's wife, said as we stood looking into the parsonage fireplace. The embers from the evening before had long since burned out, leaving a pile of cold gray ashes. "But it wasn't the spirits that scared us—they weren't aggressive or threatening. It was the experience itself that frightened us—the fact that we'd never before seen or heard or had anything like it happen. I mean, when it first happened, we all ran out of the room. But then we came back in, a couple of us at a time, until we were all in the room again."

"Did the ghosts—there were four, I believe you said—did they reappear?" I asked.

"I'm not sure they ever *dis*appeared," Mrs. Halliday said. "At least not while the fire was going. When we came back into the room, they were still where we'd last seen them."

"In the flames?" Devaney said.

"Yes. In the flames."

"Did they speak?" I asked. "Earlier you said you *heard*."

"And what did they look like?" Devaney said.

The pastor's wife gestured toward the huge stone fireplace. The opening stood nearly six feet high and six feet wide, with a beehive oven built into the left side.

"The kids had piled plenty of wood on it, so the flames were pretty high. We were reading a Bible passage—about Daniel in the fiery furnace, of all things—when suddenly we heard faint voices, squeaky, distant voices. At first I thought it was hissing logs—you know how they sound. But one of the children said, "Look. There's somebody in there, in the fire!' We all looked and, sure enough, there was a face—a man's face—with a long beard. It was like he was part of the flames, and his image rippled and distorted as the flames moved, kind of the way an image moves when you disturb the surface of a pond. He seemed to be calling for help—his mouth was moving urgently, but we couldn't really make out what he was saying."

"But weren't there four of them?" Devaney said.

"Yes. A moment later a woman appeared, then two young boys, teenagers or younger."

"Were they dressed in suits, work clothes, anything with color?" I asked.

"They were the way people look in school portraits—head or head-and-shoulders shots. I don't remember any color, but my impression was that I was seeing black-and-white Civil War photos, like tintypes or daguerreotypes of famous generals. Not with uniforms, I'm just saying I was reminded of that era."

"Did they fade? How long did you sit and watch them?" I asked.

"They faded as the fire burned down. They might have stayed longer if the fire had kept going, I suppose,

but we were afraid to throw more wood on it. As for how long—from the time we first saw them and ran out of the room until the time they disappeared—that must have been about an hour and a half."

Devaney shot a couple of pictures of the fireplace and the room.

"Anything else you can add?" I said. "Any theory on what they wanted?"

"Mr. Hoag," the pastor's wife said. "Late last night I phoned my husband at the conference he's attending. When I told him about it, he said it was probably a case of mass hysteria, that all thirteen of us were predisposed to a group experience like it because we'd come from the cemetery. I reminded him *I hadn't gone to the cemetery*, but he ignored that. He wasn't here. I was. And I believe someone—*four* someones—tried to communicate with us last night. I don't believe it was a hallucination or hysteria. I plan to light the fire again tonight, Mr. Hoag, and if you and Mr. Devaney would like to come by and visit after supper, I'd be happy to have your company."

Devaney nodded his head, so I accepted for us, thanked her, and we all agreed on seven o'clock.

Andy and Diane Hermann, the youth group advisors we interviewed at four, added nothing to Mrs. Halliday's story. Rather than use the term *ghosts*, they spoke of the four faces in the flames as *spirits*. Like the minister's wife, they too stressed that while this new experience itself had unnerved them at first, once they "warmed to the spirits," to use Andy's words, they could see the visitors meant no harm. The Hermanns agreed that the four spirits seemed desperate to communicate some warning message, and both Andy and Diane were sorry they couldn't interpret it. We didn't tell them we'd be returning to the parsonage that night to sit by the fireplace with Mrs. Halliday. I wondered if they'd find out and show up.

The other youth group advisors, Bob and Danielle Cassidy, spoke of the apparitions as *entities*. Their story jived with the ones we'd already heard. They did, however, add two bits of new information.

"All four of the entities seemed to be mouthing the same thing, the same couple of words," Danielle recalled.

"She's right," Bob said. "I'm sure they were all trying to say the same thing. They looked like that famous ghoulish painting of someone trying to scream."

"I think it's called *The Scream*," Devaney said, and the couple nodded.

"Any idea what they might have been trying to say?" I said.

"Bob and I don't," Danielle said. "But two girls in our youth group, Clarissa and Shawna Jones—their father is Clarence Jones, the new professor of Black History at Dartmouth—thought they heard what the entities were saying. The family just moved up from South Carolina."

"What did the girls think the ghosts—excuse me, *entities*—were saying?" I said.

"*Chambers*," she said. "They both thought the entities were saying *chambers*."

"What are they—lip readers?" Devaney said. "How'd they make out what the ghosts were saying?"

"They *heard* them," Danielle said. "Both girls said they heard them."

"And did the girls think *chambers* meant a place—like in the judge's chambers," I asked. "Or was it somebody's last name, with a capital C?"

Bob and Danielle shrugged.

ℭℭℭ

While we were home grabbing a quick supper before our return to Mrs. Halliday's, I called our friend Dutch Roberts, the Norwich Constable, hoping he'd be able to

shed some light on the mystery. His wife Patsy said he and his brother-in-law were out for their usual Sunday evening of bowling.

"He'll be home around nine-thirty," she said. "Do you want me to have him call you then, Hoag, or will it wait until morning?"

"Tonight, if he doesn't mind," I said.

"Is it about the parsonage ghosts?"

"Yeah. How'd you guess?"

"Elementary, my dear Hoag, elementary," Patsy said. "Everybody's talking about it. Dutch took a phone report last night and scooted around the corner to the parsonage right after it happened. But the fire had died down by the time he got there, and the so-called ghosts were long gone."

"Did he interview the kids? The twin girls?"

"Yes. They said they heard the four ghosts say *chambers*. But none of the others heard it. They only saw lips moving."

"And what did Dutch conclude?"

"Nothing. He has no explanation. But there was no threat, no apparent danger, so he's not worried about it."

"And what about them saying *chambers*? Has he got any idea what that means?"

"Not yet. I'll have him call you when he gets in, though I doubt he'll have anything to add to what I just told you."

I thanked Patsy, then called Directory Assistance and got the new listing for Clarence Jones, the Dartmouth professor. After the fourth ring a man with a slight Southern drawl picked up. I told him who I was and asked if I could meet with him and his daughters, Clarissa and Shawna, the next evening. He was reluctant at first, but I was persistent without being pushy, promising I'd take only fifteen minutes of their time. He finally agreed and gave me directions to the condo he was renting near the college in Hanover. We set the meeting for six-thirty Monday. After I hung up, Devaney and I grabbed coffee and a couple of apple turnovers for the road and headed for the meeting with the minister's wife.

Mrs. Halliday showed us in and lit the fire in the parsonage fireplace.

"I've got fresh decaffeinated coffee and homemade tollhouse cookies," she said, turning back toward the kitchen. "I'll be right back." The woman was so nice, neither Devaney nor I had the heart to admit we'd already had dessert and coffee.

We looked around. Everything appeared the same as when we were there at three o'clock. The fire caught on fast, racing through a very dry pile of kindling Mrs. Halliday had used to start it. Before she got back with the coffee and cookies, we had a roaring blaze. Devaney and I stared into it, half-expecting to see the four ghostly visages appear.

"If they decide to appear," Mrs. Halliday said softly as she entered the room, "I'm certain they'll seem quite clear to you. This isn't like a children's magazine with a hidden picture in the scene. Either they'll appear or they won't."

"Are you saying you've seen them before?" Devaney said. "Before last night, I mean?"

She sat on a flowered Victorian side chair and set a tray on the coffee table between us.

"Strangely, no, even though we've lived in this house for eight years. That was my first time. But I knew about them. Apparently a few of the past ministers and their families saw them. They've never revealed themselves to outsiders, though, like parishioners, only to the clergy families. And until these two girls last night, no one had ever heard them, so far as I know. They'd only seen them. One minister wrote in the records that he'd been losing his hearing and developed a facility for reading lips. He

saw them a number of times and believed they were saying *jaybird*."

"So the girls' claim that the voices were saying *chambers* makes sense," I said. "*Jaybird. Cham-bers*. I can see how that minister might mistake them."

"Or maybe the girls are wrong," Devaney said, "and that minister was right. Maybe it *is* jaybird. Or *jail bird*. How far back do these sightings go?"

"Well," said Mrs. Halliday. "The man who believed they were mouthing *jaybird* was here in the early 1900s. One parsonage journal from a different minister had an entry about the apparitions—not what they were *saying*, just about their presence—around 1870."

"Do you mind if we take a look at the written documentation?" Devaney said, sounding very professional.

"Not at all. I figured you'd want to examine it, so I have it laid out on the dining room table."

"Devaney?" I said. "Take your camera. I'll watch the fire."

My father-in-law grabbed his camera and went with Mrs. Halliday to shoot the written material. No sooner had he left than the fire flared up. Four faces appeared in the flames, their mouths working like fish gasping for air. Sure enough, all four seemed to be mouthing either *jaybird* or *chambers*, though I couldn't distinguish which. Nor could I hear anything. I felt myself blinking and could hear my brain telling me this had to be an illusion, a magic trick, but I couldn't look away. I didn't feel frightened, and I was more entranced than anything. Something about the way they looked told me that these four souls—or entities or spirits—were clearly a minister, his wife, and two children. Five minutes later when the door opened and Devaney and Mrs. Halliday came back into the room, the four vanished.

"You okay, Hoag?" Devaney said. "You look a little washed out."

"I saw them," I said. "Just as the others said."

Devaney looked at the fireplace, then aimed his camera at it and shot a frame.

"They're gone," I said. "They didn't wait for the fire to burn down. They disappeared when you two came in. Maybe you startled them."

"What'd they say?" he asked.

"Just what the others told us. They seemed to be saying either *jaybird* or *chambers*, but I'm not certain. It could've been something else, but I had a preconceived idea what it would be, so that's all I could see the lips saying."

The three of us sat watching the fire for another half hour, eating cookies and drinking coffee, waiting for an encore. Nothing happened. I wondered whether the presence of Devaney's camera made a difference, but even after we moved the camera into another room, they didn't show again. Finally, just as we got up to leave, the fire flared unexpectedly. No one appeared, there was just the flare-up. I wrote in my notebook that, although it was probably nothing, the flare-up could have been an acknowledgment, or perhaps a goodnight.

Dutch Roberts phoned right after I got home.

"You actually saw them?" he said. "Aw, Hoag, you're kidding, right?"

I assured him I was dead serious.

"So what do you know about all this?" I said. "Tell me new stuff, stuff I don't already know, anything—besides Saturday night's incident—that may seem a little weird. You know, past history, other Norwich spook stories, reports of ghosts or apparitions."

"As a matter of fact," he said, "there is one report that's come up time and again for decades. It's tied to the River Bend Cemetery where the kids were before they saw the fireplace ghosts."

"Is this the story about walkers being drawn to the cemetery?" I said. It was one I'd heard several times over the years.

"Yeah, that's it," Dutch said. "I'll bet I've had forty or fifty people tell me almost the same story—sane, respectable pillars of the community, too, not just winos and wackos."

"They're walking past the cemetery at night," I said, "and something inexplicably draws them in. Then whatever has led them there disappears. Right?"

"Basically, yes. It leads them, or *they* lead them—some reports tell of two, three, or four spirits. Put it this way—*the guiding force* draws them to the oldest part of the cemetery."

"And disappears?"

"Yes. Once the guiding force gets them there, it leaves them standing."

"Anybody been able to describe the apparitions?" I said.

"No. It's like they had more of a sense of whatever it was. A couple of them said it was a faintly glowing shape, like a big drop of water with light shining through it, or through *them*—one lady saw four."

"And like the fireplace ghosts, there was never any attempt to frighten or harm, correct?"

"Correct," Dutch said.

"Did any of them describe the four spirits—or giant water droplets, or whatever they saw—in a way that sounds like the four fireplace images I saw?"

"Tell you what, Hoag. Why don't you and Devaney come by the office tomorrow morning around eight. I'll have coffee. You guys bring a bag of Danish pastries and I'll let you look over all the past reports. There's a few photos of the sites, too—not of the spooks, just where the incidents occurred. You can get names, addresses, and numbers if you want to interview anybody."

I told Dutch we'd see him around eight, then called Devaney about it, undressed and climbed into bed.

"I'd want to know more about the past ministers who lived in that parsonage," Carol said, as I was lying with my eyes open. "Maybe then you can learn whether the faces were a minister and family."

I made a mental note to call Mrs. Halliday for information. Even if she didn't know, she'd have old records and could put me in touch with her church historian. With Devaney's background as a history teacher, he'd love poring over historical documents.

☾☾☾

Dutch Roberts was at his desk when we walked in the next morning. The wall clock said 7:55. Devaney plunked the bag of Danish pastries down on Dutch's desk blotter.

"There's breakfast," Devaney said. "Coffee ready?"

Dutch motioned toward a counter against the wall. "Our most reliable employee, Mr. Coffee, is on the job," he said, and the popping, gurgling, and perking noises started. "I already drank one pot. Been making copies for you guys since seven-thirty." He placed two manila folders on the desk in front of us.

Devaney and I plopped down in the visitor chairs facing the desk. We ignored the folders for the moment and small-talked until the coffee was ready, then fixed ourselves a mug each and sat back down.

"That folder has the notes on the different River Bend incidents," Dutch said. "It wasn't hard to come up with, because myself and my three predecessors kept a separate file on the cemetery. Whenever we had an incident, it not only went down in the general reports, but we slipped a carbon in that special file. Everett Carlson started it back in the 1920s. I can't give

you any of the photos, because they're originals, but you can look over the originals while you're here and take the black-and-white photocopies with you. The other folder is names, addresses, and phone numbers of people involved. I couldn't give you any reports on the parsonage ghosts, because this is the first I've heard of it. I guess ministers and their families wouldn't talk about it or didn't call it in. Not a conspiracy, just that folks probably didn't want to appear insane or be laughed at."

"Or accused of consorting with the devil," Devaney added.

"Thanks for the folders, Dutch," I said. "We'll look them over at home. But boil it down for us. What's your take on the River Bend stories?"

Devaney began shuffling through the original photos.

"There's too many reports from too many credible people to not think there's something going on," Dutch said. "There's something magnetic about that back section of the graveyard. Not magnetic in the lodestone sense, but in the weird sense. People say they're drawn to it. That's *their* words. *Drawn to it*. From what I've gleaned out of the reports—the older ones and mine—they don't really *see* anything. There's no substance. Some suggest swamp gas, others say pranksters. Myself, I've never seen or felt anything in there—and I've gone and sat or stood there for hours. Many nights, when things were slow, I'd park my patrol car in River Bend, drink coffee and read the paper. Nothing. But I don't discount what so many others say has happened. Ghosts, spirits, energy? I don't know. But it's something."

"And what about the parsonage fireplace and those twin girls in the youth group?" I said.

"Oh, the Jones girls? Yeah, *chambers*. Hoagie, I

haven't a clue on that one. That was the first report on that house, so I've only just now started a file."

"You think the parsonage and the cemetery incidents are related?" I said. "Same ghosts or different ones?"

Dutch shrugged. "Dunno. You suggesting the ghosts have migrated—from haunting the cemetery to haunting the house?"

"No," I said. "Mrs. Halliday says the fireplace ghosts have been there for over a hundred years. It's just that this is the first you've heard of them."

"The kids were at the River Bend Cemetery," Dutch said. "They saw ghosts that night at the parsonage, but not at the cemetery. Could be the same ghosts, or—" Dutch caught himself and laughed. "Geez, Hoag, you've got me doing it now—talking about these ghosts, spirits, entities, whatever, as if they're real, a proven fact. You two may be ready to fall into it, but as an officer of the law I've got to remain a skeptic, stick with hard evidence."

"Then you've already tried a Geiger counter?" Devaney said, glancing up from the photos.

Dutch Roberts grinned sheepishly. "Yeah, about four years ago. No radiation."

"It was worth a shot," Devaney said, grinning back.

We finished off the pastries and coffee, thanked our old friend, and walked outside and around the corner to the church office to meet with Mrs. Halliday and Arthur Lambert, the church historian. We spent the rest of the morning examining the church's historical documents.

"So the parsonage is on the site of one that burned to the ground in 1858," Devaney said on the ride home. "With Reverend Nightingale, his wife, and two sons inside. You think the fireplace ghosts are the Nightingales?"

"Could be," I said. "The newspaper clippings of the time suggest it was arson."

"Suspected, but never proven," Devaney said. "Makes sense, though. The guy had no shortage of detractors and no shortage of enemies. Reverend Nightingale was outspoken on many issues including gambling, alcohol, child labor, the treatment of Indians, and slavery. He was very well known in abolitionist circles."

"Tomorrow we'll check town and cemetery records, see if a contemporary of Nightingale's—someone with a name like Chambers—died in the years after the fire."

We spent the afternoon in my kitchen, going over Dutch's file of the River Bend incidents. There was a remarkable consistency to the stories, and a hundred years of passersby seemed drawn to the same part of the old burying ground.

"You think the later ones knew about the earlier ones?" Devaney said. "If none of the people knew about the others' stories, maybe you'd have something. But who says they didn't find out about the earlier stories and report the same thing—whether it really happened or not? What's to stop us from doing it ourselves?"

"We'll find out tonight. We can stop by River Bend Cemetery after we meet with the Jones twins. In the meantime, I'll look over the name-and-address file. You see if you can work out a grid, a calendar, of the cemetery appearances. See if there's a pattern."

"You mean like full moons?" Devaney quipped. "Appearances by Halley's Comet, Pisces-Virgo rising, stuff like that?"

"Whatever you can manage. You're welcome to use the computer in my room if you need the Internet, or the National Weather Service, or the Oceanographic Institute."

"Or Dionne Warwick's Psychic Network," he said. "Hoagie, I was just kidding about that astronomy stuff."

"I know you were," I said. "But once in awhile you stumble on a good idea. Maybe this is one of them. Check it out. Could be something there."

I doubted he'd turn up anything, but one never knew. After all, tracking the blue moon had helped us in the case of the secret graves at the French Acre. Besides, this would keep him out of my hair while I sneaked in a forty-minute nap on my recliner.

I heard him returning and was able to look awake when he walked back into the room. For all I knew, he'd caught a few winks himself in my study.

"Nothing," Devaney said. "How about you?"

I looked down. I had the name-and-address folder on my lap. The incident folder was on the coffee table. But here was an *incident report* staring up at me—from the *name-and-address* folder. It was an original, not a copy. I scanned it quickly. It wasn't one we'd seen.

"Just this," I said, holding up the report. "When Dutch did his photocopying this morning, he must have misfiled this incident report. It's an original."

"So spill it," Devaney said. "What's there?"

"In July 1985, a Dartmouth College student and her boyfriend biked to the cemetery in late afternoon to do a couple of charcoal gravestone rubbings. When they finished, they rode to Dan & Whit's Store to buy sandwiches. But they forgot one of the rubbings and biked back to River Bend. They weren't drawn inside, as others had been, but the woman had an experience."

"Like what? Did they see the ghosts?"

"No, they didn't. Neither the girl nor her boyfriend saw a thing. But the girl reported hearing a whispery voice. It drew her to the same spot the others were drawn."

"So the *voice* drew her, not the visions, not some magnetic feeling," Devaney said. "Does it say what she

heard, what the voice said? Was it one voice or four? The twins heard four at the parsonage, didn't they? Did this cemetery voice say *jaybird*? Or maybe *chambers*?"

"The report doesn't say. But we've got her name. Let's call her and ask."

"She was a college student," Devaney said. "The address is probably a dorm. I'll bet she's moved out of the area long ago, got married and has a different last name now."

"We'll check the Alumnae Affairs Office," I said. "If we can't locate her by computer, we can call the office on campus and sweet-talk them."

I pulled the paper clip off the report. Two Polaroid instant pictures fell onto the desk. They'd been clipped underneath.

"What're those?" Devaney said, sliding around beside me to look.

The first, like the others we'd seen in Dutch's office, appeared to be a nighttime shot taken in the oldest section of the cemetery. The flash hadn't helped much, but there were enough similarities to the other pictures that we knew it showed the same basic area. The second had been taken in an office, probably the Town Constable's. The names on the back of the photo matched the names in the report. This was the college student who had heard the voice, and her male friend.

"*She's black.*" The words popped out of Devaney's mouth before he could think. Amazingly, although the report had been written in the 1980s, it had not described her race. Her male friend was white.

"And your point is?" I said.

"I don't know that I had a point," Devaney said. "It just jumped out at me." He stared silently at the photo for a moment. "The Jones twins are black, too."

"I have no idea if that means anything," I said. "But you're right."

We tried to puzzle it out for five minutes and got nowhere, so Devaney went to the computer to track down the former college student through Alumnae Affairs. In less than fifteen minutes he had her address and phone number.

"Bingo!" Devaney said. "She lives in California now. She and her husband teach at UCLA. She teaches Theater. I've got her home and office phone numbers."

I placed a call to her home number first and left a message on her answering machine, asking her to call me back collect after her suppertime. Since we were three hours ahead, Devaney and I would surely be home from interviewing the Jones twins by then. Then I tried her office at the university and was surprised to have her pick up.

"Dr. Diana Hanley?" I asked, and when she said yes, I explained the reason for my call. She had only five minutes left on her lunch break, and gave me a quick recap of the incident at River Bend Cemetery the evening she'd gone grave rubbing.

"Exactly what did you hear?" I asked. "The report doesn't make it clear except to say you heard a whisper. Was it a single voice?"

"Pretty sure it was one voice—a man's. And not exactly a whisper, but a deep, scratchy, hoarse sort of whisper—like someone gasping for air or someone thirsting for water. Croaky."

"Croaky?" I said.

"Yeah. Someone in distress, like a death scene in a World War II movie. You know, the dying soldier cradled in his buddy's arms on the battlefield. A weak voice, fading, croaky."

"And what did the voice say?" I asked.

"*Nazareth*, maybe. At least, that's what I think it said. It wasn't perfectly clear. Like I said, the voice was weak. But I'm pretty sure it said *Nazareth*. Or possibly *Naz-rus*."

"*Nazareth*? As in *Jesus of*?"

"I don't know if it's Nazareth. As I said, it could have been *Naz-rus*. It's been a lot of years since then."

"You're sure the voice didn't come from pranksters hiding behind a tombstone?" I said. "You know, from other college kids?"

"Positive," she said. "Nor did it come from inside my head."

"But the police report states that your friend, who was standing beside you, didn't hear any voice at all."

"That's correct, he didn't. But I did."

"Just *Nazareth*? That's all the voice said?"

"That's it. And not necessarily *Nazareth*. My *first* impression was that the voice said *Naz-rus*. Just *Naz-rus*. Over time I've started to think maybe it was Nazareth, but initially I'm pretty sure I heard *Naz-rus*. Might have even been *Az-rus*, for all I know. I remember thinking afterwards that I wasn't even sure I'd heard the N."

"Any chance it was a dialect, somebody saying *Nazareth* in a way that came out *Naz-rus*?"

"Can't say," she said.

There was nothing else Dr. Hanley could tell me, and I couldn't think of anything else to ask, so I thanked her for talking with me and hung up.

At 6:20 Devaney and I pulled up in front of a lovely condo near Dartmouth College. We wanted to arrive a little early, since the twins' father had said we could only have fifteen minutes of their time. If we were going to grab a little extra time, it'd probably be easier to sneak it in on the front end of the visit.

"Quite the place, ain't it?" Devaney said as I pressed the doorbell. "Now I can see where that expression came from—*keeping up with the Joneses*."

I shook my head and offered my father-in-law my weakest smile.

Two minutes later we were sitting on a comfortable sofa opposite Clarence and Celia Jones and their girls,

Clarissa and Shawna. We asked them to tell us what happened at the parsonage on Saturday night. Their version, which took about ten minutes, matched those of Mrs. Halliday and the four advisors. I was glad we'd picked up the extra time on the front end of the interview.

"But you were the only two who heard voices, right?" I asked.

The girls nodded.

"They were trying to shout to us, but they sounded like people yelling from a faraway hilltop," one of them said.

"And it was like all four of their voices could barely make up one whole voice," the other said. "It took a lot out of them."

"But you two *heard* them, right?" Devaney said. "You didn't just read their lips?"

"Oh, we heard 'em, all right," Shawna said.

"And you're sure of what they said?" I asked.

The two girls screwed their mouths into identical funny faces and said, "*Chambers*, I think."

"Anything else?" Devaney asked.

"That's all."

"How about your visit to the cemetery?" I said. "See or hear anything at River Bend Cemetery? Or on the walk there or back?"

The girls' eyes grew wide as they turned to look at each other.

"We were just talking about that," Clarissa said.

"We didn't hear or see anything," Shawna said. "But we *sensed* something."

Their father leaned forward on his seat. "This is the first mention of that," he said. "What did you sense?"

"Clarence's grandmother had the Sight," Celia Jones whispered to us.

"We didn't see any spirits or ghosts or anything," Shawna said. "But we felt a pull, for sure."

"Someone wanted us to come closer," Clarissa said.

"And what did you do?" their father said.

"We walked in a different direction," Shawna said.

"We steered the rest of the group away from it," her sister said.

"Were you afraid?" I asked.

"Not for us. But we didn't know about the others," she said.

"What others? Other spirits?" Devaney said.

"No. The other kids," she continued. "The kids in the Youth Group, we were afraid for them and for Mr. and Mrs. Hermann and Mr. and Mrs. Cassidy."

"And not spirits, just spirit, one force drawing us," she said.

Her sister nodded.

"And was it different from the four faces and voices in the fireplace?" I asked.

The twins looked at each other, then nodded. They seemed certain.

"What part of the cemetery were you feeling drawn to?" Devaney asked. "Pretend you're walking with us through the front gate. Describe it for us."

I knew Devaney wanted to ask the twins if they'd be willing to go to River Bend with us—I was dying to ask them, too—but we both knew the father wouldn't allow it.

The girls not only described it, they drew a map on a sheet of notebook paper. The place they had stopped to divert their group was just short of the path entering the oldest part of the cemetery, the area in all the incident reports.

Professor Jones had begun looking at his watch, and I could see from the grandfather clock behind him that it was 6:45. Our time was up. I thanked the Joneses for their time and we eased toward the front door. The question still burned inside me, and apparently it still burned in Devaney, who surprised me by pulling an old Peter Falk/Colombo detective's trick.

"Dr. Jones, I know this would be a terrible imposition," he said abashedly. "I know you and your family are very busy, and this has been quite an ordeal. But . . ." Then he shook his head and looked away. "Oh, never mind," he said.

"What is it, Mr. Devaney?" the professor said, taking the bait. "Is there some way I can help?"

Devaney turned back and looked Jones right in the eye. "I don't suppose you and your wife and the girls—in the daylight, not at night, of course—I don't suppose you and your family would go back there with us, would you? With me and Hoag? You see, me and Hoag, we don't have the Sight. But maybe you do. Or your girls."

Devaney held the eye contact, and I thought I saw Jones cave a little. But I was wrong.

"I don't think so, Mr. Devaney. I'd rather not put the girls through such an ordeal. They knew enough to steer clear of it once, so I think we'll go along with their good sense. It's nice of you to invite us along, though. Good night."

Devaney didn't say a word as we passed through the Dartmouth Campus and drove downhill toward the Ledyard Bridge over the Connecticut River. As the crow flies it's less than two miles from the center of Hanover, New Hampshire to the center of Norwich, Vermont.

"It was a darned good try," I said finally. "I was itching to ask him, too, but couldn't figure a way to lead into it."

"Nothing short of brilliant, you say?"

I looked across at my father-in-law in the passenger seat. He was grinning like a Cheshire cat.

"Just a tad bit short of brilliant," I said. "If it had worked—well . . ."

"Then you'd have conceded: nothing short of brilliant," he finished.

"Maybe," I said. "I guess he watched *Columbo*, too."

I picked up Route 5 and followed it north past the Congregational Church and the school.

"So we're going ghost busting, eh?" Devaney said.

I turned in at the gate of the River Bend Cemetery and parked about twenty feet in. I grabbed my flashlight from the glove box and we got out.

"Should've packed my piece," Devaney said, patting his right hip, then his left armpit. Devaney didn't own a gun. As far as I knew, the man had never even hunted deer or rabbits.

I held the twins' map in front of me and shone the light on it.

"We should've come by and checked it out in daylight," Devaney said. "We knew from Dutch's files where to look."

"Shhh," I said.

"Why're we stopping?" Devaney whispered. "You hear something?"

"No," I said. "But let's see if we can sense anything. See if we feel the pull."

We didn't. So we proceeded slowly, stopping every twenty or thirty feet to check again. Nothing. Eventually we got to the point where the twins had felt the force before they steered their youth group away. We stood still and waited quietly a full minute.

"Where's Charlie Rivers when you need him?" Devaney finally said.

Charlie Rivers, an Abenaki Indian in his seventies, had been one of the last of the old-time apple-branch dowsers. We'd helped him clear brush at the French Acre. His dowsing skills had applied to more than locating water, and Devaney was right—there wouldn't be anybody more helpful than Charlie at the River Bend Cemetery—except maybe the Jones twins.

We walked into the oldest section of the cemetery, but felt no "presence." Nothing *drew* us, or *pulled* us, or *summoned* us. Devaney and I simply didn't possess the Sight, not in the way Charlie and the twins did. I shone my flashlight on a few gravestones. Nothing. We turned around and headed for the car.

"Come one, Charlie," I said, calling up toward the heavens. "How about a break, old buddy? After all that brush we helped you clear?"

No answer. No clap of thunder or bolt of lightning to illuminate a grave. We walked on.

"Hey, look," Devaney said, pointing at my car.

Directly in front of it stood a deer. I shone my flashlight on it, but it didn't move. When I took the beam off it, it started *toward* us. We backed off of the narrow dirt drive and watched it amble past us, coming within three feet. I could have reached out and touched it. We followed it. A minute later we were back at the same place we'd been earlier, at the entrance to the oldest part of the cemetery.

The deer kept going. We followed ten paces behind. It wended its way among the graves, gravitating toward the farthest corner, eventually stopping. It had led us to a huge flat weathered stone. It looked as if it measured four feet wide by eight feet long, perhaps six inches thick. The stone must have weighed several tons.

"That's what they call a wolf lid or a wolf stone," Devaney said. "They put those on top in Colonial days so the wolves couldn't dig up the bodies."

"I've heard of them," I said. "And seen a few, too, mostly down in Connecticut, around Stonington and Mystic. But they're mostly two or three feet wide by six feet long, two or three inches thick. This one's more than

a plain old wolf stone, Devaney. I think it must be the cover to a mausoleum."

I shone a light on it.

"It's worn," Devaney said. "But I think it says *Masters.*" He rubbed a hand over the stone's faded letters. "I was hoping it'd say *Chambers.*"

"Yeah, me too. But the deer clearly led us here, didn't it?" I said.

"Yeah, it did," Devaney answered. "Hey, where'd it go?"

The deer was nowhere to be seen.

"Think it was Charlie?" I said.

"Three Rivers?" my father-in-law said. "Could've been. But even if it was, and if I'd have thought to get him on film just now, a picture of a deer in a graveyard wouldn't convince anybody of anything, would it?" He whistled a few eerie notes from *The Twilight Zone* and we walked back to the car.

☾☾☾

The next morning we checked out plot maps for Norwich cemeteries, including River Bend. We found the notation for the plot the deer had led us to: *Masters family: James Masters 1747-1809 and wife Grace (nee Roberts) Masters 1754-1818, their daughter Rebecca 1777-1781, their son Albert Masters 1786-1852 and his wife Jenny (nee Russell) Masters 1793-1816 who died in childbirth with son Robert Masters 1816-1816. Albert's second wife Alice (nee Burns) Masters_1801-1851.* In small print in the margin someone had added: *Grace (nee Masters 1820) Nightingale buried with her family 1858 at North Cemetery, Norwich.*

"Nightingale!" Devaney exclaimed. "Same as the minister in the 1858 parsonage fire."

We checked the records for the North Cemetery, a larger and slightly newer cemetery just north of River

Bend, and found the Nightingale plot on the map. All four Nightingales had died in 1858: *Reverend Frederick, wife Grace (nee Masters), son Robert, son Franklin.*

"Still no *Chambers*," Devaney said glumly.

"Not yet," I said. "But we've connected the parsonage site with the River Bend grave. Until now we had two separate and unrelated cases."

"I thought you preferred to call them *stories*," Devaney said. "I'm the one who calls them *cases*. After all, we're reporters, not ghost busters. Remember?"

ℭℭℭ

We hit Dutch's office and once again drank his coffee as we shared our Danish pastries.

"So you think the four ghosts in the fireplace are the Nightingales, the minister and family who burned in the fire in 1858," Dutch said. "And Mrs. Nightingale was Grace Masters, whose family is buried—*without her*—in the oldest section of River Bend Cemetery. And the Fireplace Four, as they'll no doubt become known after Hoagie's front-page story wins the Pulitzer, have been trying to tell us something."

"They're trying to tell somebody something," I said. "But I don't know if it's us they're trying to tell."

"Yeah," Devaney said. "It seems like only black people—I mean *people of color*—hear them. White people just *see* them, make out their lips moving."

Dutch frowned at Devaney like he was nuts.

"Where's this *only-black-people-can-hear-them* stuff coming from, Devaney?" Dutch said. "The two Jones girls heard them, and they're the only two, right?"

"And Dr. Hanley," Devaney said.

Dutch looked puzzled.

"Diana Hanley, the black Dartmouth student in your

incident files," I said. "The one who was there doing the grave-rubbings with her boyfriend."

"I know the incident," Dutch said. "How did you know she was black?"

"From the Polaroid," I said. "It was the only original photo you gave us. If it had been a photocopy like the others, we'd have never guessed. She was very light-skinned."

"I didn't give you any original," Dutch said. "I double-checked everything to make sure I retained my originals. I'm positive I only gave you photocopies of files and pictures. I never even noticed the woman was black."

Devaney shot me a funny look. His lips didn't move, and I half-expected him to start whistling *The Twilight Zone* theme song again. How had the Polaroid come our way? Myself, I was thinking: *Charlie Three Rivers.*

Dutch went to the cabinet, withdrew a file, and leafed through it as he returned to his chair.

"According to the file, Miss Hanley heard a voice saying *Nazareth* or something like that. Not *Chambers* or *jaybird.* So you've got two little girls hearing *chambers* and a college student who heard *Nazareth.* And the student heard it in a different setting—if she heard anything at all. Why assume the connection among the three who heard something is the fact that they're black? They're also all female. They're also all students. And they also all lived in Hanover, New Hampshire, have a connection with the college, and visited Norwich, Vermont. If you want to take it to extremes, they all crossed the Ledyard Bridge to get here. Maybe they're all bicycle riders, too."

I sat feeling stupid. I hadn't thought of the other common denominators.

The phone rang. Dutch answered it, looked mildly surprised. "It's for you," he said, handing me the receiver.

It was Carol, who knew where her father and I were. She had just gotten back from her morning walk to find two messages on the answering machine. One was one from Dr. Hanley, who had my number from the message I'd left on her home machine. She wanted me to call her at her office around 10:30 my time, 7:30 hers. She'd just be getting to her office then and didn't have a class until eight. The other was Clarence Jones, asking me to call his condo. Since he had only called ten minutes earlier, I asked Dutch if I could call from there.

"Mr. Hoag," Jones said on the phone. "My girls had a strange night after your visit. Not exactly nightmares, but they had weird dreams."

"Tell me about it," I said.

"They dreamed they woke up during the night because of a voice. Both girls described the same dream."

"Not the fireplace voices, but a hoarse voice, a man's, right?" I said.

"Yes. How'd you know?"

"Just a hunch. Please continue. What did the voice say?"

"They said it was sort of pleading. And they thought it said *Az-rus*."

"*Az-rus*?" I said.

"Yes, *Az-rus.*"

"Any chance it was *Nazareth*?" I said.

"I asked them that, too. They thought it was *Az-rus*. Two syllables."

"Were they frightened?"

"No. But they said they awoke feeling sad, and sorry they couldn't help."

"Anything else?" I said.

"Yes," he said. "Awhile ago my sister called from South Carolina. You'll remember my wife Celia told you last night that my grandmother had the Sight?"

"Yes. Is your grandmother still alive?" I asked.

"No. But my sister Nell seems to have it to some degree, too."

"Go on."

"She had the same dream, the same dream as the girls. Heard the same voice say the same thing."

"*Az-rus*? Or *Nazareth*?" I asked.

"*Az-rus*, I believe. She also felt the overwhelming sadness that she couldn't help whomever was calling out to her. What was different from the twins' dreams is, my sister had a sense the voice was connected to her area, South Carolina. Any ideas? What should I do?"

Dutch and Devaney could only hear my end of the conversation, and they were fit to be tied. I wanted to ask Jones again if he'd let Shawna and Clarissa go to the cemetery, but I remembered how he'd responded to Devaney's Columbo ploy. Besides, they'd already heard the voice and the word or name that Dr. Hanley had heard in 1985. They didn't need to go to the cemetery again to verify that. Nevertheless, something told me the twins visiting the cemetery again would be the key to unlocking the mystery.

"I've got another phone call to make," I said. "Can you call me around suppertime?"

"About five-thirty?" Dr. Jones said.

"That'd be great. And would you mind if I called your sister Nell and spoke directly with her about this?"

Jones gave me his sister's last name and phone number. I thanked him and hung up.

"I see from your note that his sister's last name isn't *Chambers*," Devaney said. "Or *Nazareth*."

"No such luck," I said. "But we do have another black female who heard the voice. And Dutch, she's not affiliated with Dartmouth College nor has she crossed the Ledyard Bridge." Having made my point, I filled them in on my conversation with Clarence Jones.

I left Devaney going over records at the Town offices

and library. He wanted to check all the cemeteries for any names like Chambers. He had also set up a second meeting with Arthur Lambert, the church historian, for 10:00. I told him I'd meet him at 11:00 in front of Dutch's office, then drove home to call Nell in South Carolina. The man who answered said she worked mornings, but I could catch her at noon when she got home.

At 10:30 I phoned Dr. Hanley in California. She'd had the same dream as Shawna, Clarissa, and Nell.

"I hadn't heard the voice since that evening in 1985," she said. "So this time, because it was on my mind, I listened more closely. I think it said *Lazarus*—like in the Bible. Not *Nazareth*."

I told her about the parsonage and the fireplace ghosts, gave her the basics on the twins and Dr. Jones's sister Nell hearing the voice, too. Then I asked her if *chambers* or *jaybird* made any sense to her. No luck. I asked her to call if anything else came up and promised I'd keep her updated.

I went to Carol's office and pulled her Bible and concordance off the shelf. The concordance told me where in the New Testament to find *Lazarus*. He'd been Jesus' friend, Martha and Mary's brother. The sisters second-guessed his death, wondering if Jesus of Nazareth, had he come right away when they first sent word their brother was sick, mightn't have saved Lazarus' life. When he finally did arrive and learned his dear friend was dead, Jesus wept. I remembered the line now: *Jesus wept.* It was the answer to the question: What is the shortest sentence in the Bible? *Jesus wept.* He wept for Lazarus. When Mary and Martha took Jesus to their brother's gravesite—in a foreshadowing of Jesus's own Resurrection—Jesus commanded, "Lazarus, come out!" And Lazarus did. He rose from the dead and came out.

I returned the Bible and concordance to the shelf,

went to the phone and called Clarence Jones. Answering machine. I left a message.

"Dr. Jones, this is Hoag. Is it possible that Shawna and Clarissa heard the voice saying not *Az-rus* but *Lazarus*? I'd appreciate it if you'd ask them when they get home from school. If you can't reach me or my wife Carol, please leave a message on my machine. I'll chat with you at 5:30 tonight as planned."

At 11:45 I couldn't stand to wait any longer. I called Nell, Dr. Jones's sister, in South Carolina. She answered, and in short order related the story of her dream and the voice.

"And what, exactly, did the voice say?" I asked. "Did it say *Az-rus*?"

"To tell you the truth, Mr. Hoag," Nell said. "It could have been clipped speech, even a regional dialect, maybe saying *Nazareth*—or even *Lazarus*. Plenty of people mix those two words up, not only here in the South but everywhere. And *Az-rus*, well, that doesn't make any sense now, does it?"

I told her the rest of the story, about Dr. Hanley, the Nightingale family, the fireplace ghosts, and *chambers* or *jaybird*.

"Tell me," I said. "If you were to come visit your brother, and if you happened to stop by the River Bend Cemetery, do you think the Sight would be helpful in uncovering the truth?"

"Can't say for sure," she answered. "I don't have it as strong as my grandmother did. It travels through mostly the women in our family, and it's stronger in some than in others. My and Clarence's mother, for example, didn't have it at all. The twins appear to have it, from what I can see."

"Did your grandmother's mother have it?" I asked.

"She did, but then she gave it up, refused to use it. She and her husband, my great-grandfather, they were slaves. He disappeared when he was twenty-five. Ran for freedom and was never heard from again. My great-grandmother said she foresaw a horrible death for him. She warned him, begged him not to go. But he went anyway. Promised to send someone to buy the family's freedom. But no one ever came, no one ever heard from him. After that she cursed the Sight and never used it again. At least, she never spoke of it."

No sooner had I hung up than Devaney called.

"No luck on cemetery plots with the name *Chambers*," he said. "But Arthur Lambert and I found a strong motive to suspect arson in the Nightingale fire. Not only was the Reverend Nightingale vocal in the abolitionist movement, he may also have been helping to fund the Underground Railroad that helped slaves escape the South to the free states in the North."

"Call me back in five minutes," I told Devaney, and hung up. An idea—a hunch, really—was beginning to form in my brain. I dialed Nell in South Carolina again, hoping she hadn't gone out. She answered.

"Nell, it's me again, Hoag in Vermont. When did your great-grandfather disappear?"

"Just a minute, it's in the journal," she said, and the line was quiet. I heard papers rustling.

"April of 1858," she said a moment later.

"1858?"

"Yes. 1858. According to the story passed down in the family, he left at night with a little food, the clothes on his back, and a quilt."

"A quilt?" I said.

"Yes, a quilt. It served as his bedroll, but the quilt was really a map to freedom. The squares contained different pictures and symbols. Each was a clue to the safe stops on the way North."

"The Underground Railroad?" I said.

"Yes. Why?"

"I think your great-grandfather was on his way to see Reverend Nightingale in Norwich, Vermont. But the minister and all three members of his family died in a fire, leaving your great-grandfather without anyone to make that connection."

"So, what happened to him?" Nell said.

"I don't know," I said. "I'll call you back when I have more."

A minute later Devaney called back. I told him I'd be right over to pick him up. I called Clarence Jones and caught him on his lunch break.

"Dr. Jones, I really need Shawna and Clarissa to come to the cemetery," I said. "Please. Trust me. I wouldn't ask if I didn't think it was really important."

"I don't see how it would benefit the girls," he said.

"I think it's about a relative of theirs," I said.

"A relative? Which one?"

"Your great-grandfather, the slave who disappeared. I think whoever or whatever is drawing people to the cemetery is trying to tell us what happened to your great-grandfather."

Jones was quiet on the other end. He didn't ask me to explain it further. Either he trusted me or something in his soul told him there was some truth to what I was saying.

"How about four o'clock?" he said. "The girls will be home from school by then, and Celia will be home from work."

"Devaney and I will meet you in front of the Congregational Church."

I hung up and called Dutch Roberts to say Devaney and I would buy him lunch. When he asked where, I said, "At your office. We'll pick up three deli sandwiches at Dan & Whit's on our way over. Roast beef or turkey?" Then I went to pick up Devaney.

☾☾☾

"I can't just authorize a Town backhoe to open the Masters graves," Dutch said as his mouth prepared to clamp down on the sandwich. "I'd need permission either from the descendants or from the State Medical Examiner. Geez Louise, Hoagie, you can't just go digging up people's graves on a hunch."

"I don't want to open up anyone's *grave*," I explained. "The actual graves—caskets or whatever's in there—are under the *crypt*, or the *mausoleum*, or whatever it's called. They're under that huge stone slab. We won't disturb the individuals at all. I just need a look."

"No can do," Dutch said. "If word got out, I'd be up a creek without a paddle. I could lose my job, get sued."

"Dutch," Devaney chimed in. "Think of it this way. It's not about opening a grave or exhuming a body. *It's about straightening out that historic lid that's shifted out of place.*" Devaney winked a couple times to be sure Dutch caught it, then beamed a heck of a stupid grin at Dutch. If he'd had long eyelashes, we'd have seen them flutter.

Despite the free lunch and our best cajoling, Dutch wouldn't relent. He did, however, ask if he could accompany us to the cemetery at four o'clock.

"To protect the Joneses," he said.

"From the ghost?" Devaney said.

"No. From you two," Dutch said. "Together, you're a public menace."

After lunch, the three of us scouted River Bend Cemetery, but we found nothing, saw nobody.

"Looks like the place is clean," Devaney said in a TV cop voice.

"Yeah," Dutch answered in a similar voice. "The perps must've wiped the prints."

"You overlooked one thing, gentlemen," I said.

"What's that?" Devaney said in his best Joe Friday/*Dragnet* voice.

"They left a heckuva lot of bodies behind."

☾☾☾

At four o'clock an SUV pulled up in front of the Congregational Church and Clarence Jones got out. We shook hands and I thanked him for coming.

"When I got home," Jones said, "I got your message on my answering machine—from this morning. You wanted me to ask the girls if the voice in the dream might have said *Lazarus*. They weren't sure."

The rear window of the SUV wound down and a head popped out. "Daddy, Mom wants to know if we're leaving the car here."

"Just a minute, Shawna," her father said. He looked to me for direction.

"She doesn't seem frightened," I said. "How about her sister? And your wife?"

"They're fine, I think."

"Good," I said. "Let's drive the cars to the cemetery and park just inside the entrance gate, which will block anyone else from driving in and disturbing us."

Five minutes later we were out of our cars, walking toward the oldest part of River Bend Cemetery. The twins led, I walked with Clarence and Celia, and Dutch and Devaney brought up the rear.

"This is where we felt it that night," one of the twins said. "So we got everyone to go that way." She pointed off to the left at an access road leading back toward Route 5, away from the Masters crypt.

I hadn't told them where we were going. I preferred they find their own way. Maybe the deer that Devaney and I had followed had been just a deer, and our suppositions were off base.

"Do you feel the force, girls?" Devaney said.

"This isn't *Star Wars*, Devaney," Dutch whispered loudly.

"Nothing yet," the girls said. Then, a few steps later, "Yes. It's pulling us over there." They pointed toward the Masters crypt.

A moment later we were standing in front of it.

"Here," one of the twins said. "Under that giant stone."

"Any voices?" their father asked.

The girls closed their eyes and listened. "No voices," they said in unison. "Should there be?"

"We don't know," I said. "Maybe we just need to stand here and listen awhile."

The seven of us stood quietly facing the Masters crypt. Three or four minutes passed.

"I'm feeling a bit strange," Clarence Jones said.

"Are you sick, dear?" Celia asked, supporting his forearm.

"Not sick," he said, his voice growing higher, as if he were about to faint. "Just strange. Let me sit down." He turned around and sat on the edge of the stone covering the Masters crypt.

"If you feel like you're going to pass out," Celia said, "put your head between your knees."

But Dr. Jones didn't put his head between his knees. He lay back on the stone cover.

"Do you have any chest pains?" his wife said, a hint of alarm in her voice.

As he shook his head, his cell phone rang, and Celia reached inside the breast pocket of his jacket and removed it. It rang again, and as she was about to put it to her ear, her husband moaned.

"Somebody else answer it," she said, and lobbed it to the twins, who were closest.

Dr. Jones began to shiver violently and tried to wrap

his arms around himself. His eyes rolled back in his head, only the whites showing. His lips moved, something between a gasp and a hoarse whisper, and Celia put her ear to his lips.

"It's a seizure or a heart attack," Dutch said. "Give me the phone. I'll call 911." He reached toward the girls for the cell phone. But they were talking to someone.

Clarence Jones hissed out something, a phrase or a word.

Celia leaned closer to hear. "*Laz-rus*," she said. "He's saying *Laz-rus*."

The twins stood like statues, as if in a trance themselves, then linked hands, raised them heavenward, and called out together in a loud voice, "*Jabez, come out!*" Then again they commanded, "*Jabez, come out.*"

At first I thought they'd said *Chambers*. Or *jaybird*. Their lips seemed to be pronouncing those words. But they were saying *Jabez*.

The air around us was electric with tension. Still lying on his back on the stone, Clarence Jones stretched his arm toward the closest corner of the crypt. And as he did, a vapor squeezed out of the tomb, seeping out where the lid met the sides of the crypt. I could see through it, yet it wasn't totally clear, and it eerily took the shape of a hand. For a moment the tip of Clarence's Jones' index finger strained to touch the tip of the ethereal hand's index finger. I could feel the tension in my own body, wanting him to make it, yearning on his behalf. Closer, closer.

And then they did. They touched. And I blinked—one of those involuntary blinks like when something explodes, though I don't remember any sound. Later, when we recounted the experience, none of us would recall a sound, only Clarence's hand and the ghostly hand and then when they touched, the blink. And in the moments after the blink, we all saw Clarence Jones' hand—but no other hand—hanging limply over the edge of the crypt.

"We need a doctor," Dutch said, but with Celia's help Dr. Jones was sitting up.

"What happened?" he said. He stood and swatted the dust and dirt from the seat of his pants while Celia cleaned off the back of his jacket.

The twins handed him his cell phone. "Aunt Nell in South Carolina called to tell us your great-grandfather's name—*Jabez*," one of the girls said. "She wants to talk to you."

As Dr. Jones put the phone to his ear and said hello, there—not ten yards beyond the crypt—stood a deer. It gave a quick nod of its head and bounded away through the brush.

☾☾☾

Three days later Dutch Roberts had the Town backhoe in the River Bend Cemetery to "realign the lid" on the Masters crypt. Devaney and I were there. So were Clarence Jones, his family, and his sister Nell from South Carolina. Before the backhoe realigned the stone cover, though, we got a peek inside. What we discovered, in addition to the coffins of the Masters clan, were other human remains—bones later identified as a black man's. They appeared huddled in the tattered remnant of an 1850s map-quilt. One of its squares depicted four nightingales. Beside the quilt rested an empty water jug.

Later at home, Devaney and I pieced it together this way. The Masters crypt might not have been the perfect short-term hiding place for a slave traveling the Underground Railroad, but the Nightingales' house was under scrutiny and was unavailable. So the Nightingales found an alternative. Who could imagine them hiding

Jabez Jones in the crypt of Mrs. Nightingale's ancestors, the Masters clan?

Unfortunately, an arsonist, perhaps angry with the minister for his liberal views, ruined the plan by setting fire to the minister's house, snuffing out the lives of the only four people who knew Jabez Jones' hiding place and could release him from under the heavy slab.

As Jones' wife foretold, her husband would die a horrible death. And despite the fireplace ghosts trying to tell others the trapped slave's name, and Jabez himself calling attention to his plight through the name *Lazarus*, it would take nearly a hundred fifty years before his great-grandson Clarence and twin great-great-granddaughters Shawna and Clarissa set him free.

"What about the deer?" Devaney said after I'd laid out my explanation. "You didn't explain the deer. Charlie Three Rivers?"

I shrugged. "Don't know," I said. "Sometimes a deer is just a deer."

"And sometimes," Devaney said, "it's more."

I whistled a few notes from *The Twilight Zone*.

ℂℂℂ

Three months later, after the Vermont State Forensics Team released the bones, the Jones clan gathered in a South Carolina cemetery for a very belated funeral.

Devaney and I drove down for it.

The stone was simple.

JABEZ JONES
1833-1858
A FREE MAN

www.burtcreations.com

ORDER FORM

Burt Creations

PLEASE SEND ME THE FOLLOWING:

QUAN.	ITEM	PRICE
______	**A Christmas Dozen** Hard Cover Book ($17.95)	________
_____	**A Christmas Dozen** Paperback Book ($14.95)	________
_____	**A Christmas Dozen** Double cassette ($15.95)	________
_____	**A Christmas Dozen** Double CD ($16.95)	________
_____	**Unk's Fiddle** Paperback ($13.95)	________
____	**Odd Lot** Paperback Book ($14.95)	________
____	**Even Odder** Paperback Book ($14.95)	________
____	**Oddest Yet** Paperback Book ($14.95)	________
____	**Wicked Odd** Paperback Book ($14.95)	________
____	**Odd/Even/Oddest/Wicked** Four Pack ($54.80)	________

Shipping & handling is $4.50 first item, $2.50 per additional item. Connecticut residents add 6% sales tax.

SALES TAX ________

SHIPPING ________

TOTAL ________

FREE SHIPPING ON ORDERS OF MORE THAN 10 UNITS

NAME

ADDRESS

CITY STATE ZIP

TELEPHONE FAX EMAIL

PAYMENT:

❑ Checks payable to: **Burt Creations**
Mail to: 29 Arnold Place, Norwich, CT 06360

❑ VISA ❑ MasterCard

Cardnumber:______________________________

Name on card:____________________________

Exp. Date: ________(mo) ________(year)

■ **Toll free order phone** 1-866-MyDozen (866-693-6936 / Secure message machine) Give mailing/shipping address, telephone number, MC/Visa name & card number plus expiration date.

■ **Secure Fax orders:** 860-889-4068. Fill out this form & fax.

■ **On-line orders:** www.burtcreations.com
order@burtcreations.com

www.burtcreations.com